My Stepbrother, My Roommate

by

Ashley Sands

Chapter 1

Willow

"How about this one?" Madison, my best friend, asked.

I looked at the profile of the woman in the picture. She seemed kind enough, professional looking. The room seemed a bit small, but I knew I couldn't be too picky.

"She has kind eyes," I said.

"I guess that's a good thing, but aren't you more interested in how the room looks? The location?" Madison asked me.

We had been looking at a room for me to rent in Los Angeles for the last two hours. I had been offered a job as a paralegal in the area. While I could commute to work, I knew it would take about two hours every day from my current place, living with Madison. As much as I didn't want to leave her, I knew it was better to find something closer to work. I didn't want to rent my own place. As much because I couldn't afford it, and also because I wasn't sure if I was going to like the job and didn't want to be stuck in a lease if I left.

"She's a non-smoker."

"Wait, does she have a cat?" I asked.

"Shoot, she does. You could always just take allergy medicine," Madison offered.

"Not every day. It wouldn't work," I said with a sigh and closed her listing.

"Okay, so we keep looking."

"This guy looks cute," she said as she opened up the next listing.

"I'm not looking for someone cute. I'm looking for someone clean, hopefully, travels, so they are never home, doesn't smoke, doesn't have a cat and doesn't like to party until all hours of the morning."

"You would think that would be easy to find," Madison said.

I had thought the same thing, but I had only found two people that I would even consider contacting. I was beginning to wonder if I would ever find a roommate.

"Wait," I said as I looked closer at the picture of the guy. "I know him."

"Really? Care to introduce us?" she asked.

I clicked on the profile and got the first name. Jay. It said he was twenty-five, looking for a roommate from ages twenty-two to ninety. He was offering up a furnished bedroom with a shared bathroom. Large kitchen and living room and a beautiful backyard. It stated he didn't smoke, kept normal professional hours, rarely partied and considered himself clean. The pictures of the room were more beautiful than I had seen in the other places. It had a large queen bed, with still plenty of space. There was a lot of natural light and the windows looked out into the mountains and the backyard.

There was something about his look, even in the small profile picture that seemed familiar. I couldn't place it yet, I had a nagging feeling that I knew him, but I wasn't sure how.

"I think you should message him and see about meeting. Plus, the other two you liked," Madison said.

"Yeah. I will," I said. I had been dragging my feet about finding a place to live and getting a roommate. I was excited about the job and living in a new town. I wasn't looking forward to leaving Madison behind and not seeing her every day. We had lived together since we had been paired up in college. Most of my adult life had been spent with her. It was odd to think that this part of our lives was coming to an end.

"I'll go with you if that will make you feel better," she said.

"No. But thank you. I need to do this on my own. And the last thing I want is someone thinking you're their possible new roommate and them being disappointed when they get me," I said.

"That would never happen. You're the best friend and roommate ever. Anyone will be lucky to have you. Now come on. Let's see if you can meet them."

It was later in the day that I pulled up to the small cottage right outside of Los Angeles. The place wasn't very big and I wasn't even sure how it would fit two bedrooms much less the spacious living room and kitchen the pictures showed. The house did look better maintained than the one I had just left. That one had looked like it would fall down with a small wind storm. The inside hadn't been much better, as the place was full of clutter and the bedroom that she was offering up to me looked like it needed to new paint and the furniture looked older than me. The woman, Leslie, had been nice enough but I knew as soon as I walked into the place that it wasn't going to work out.

As I looked at the next place, I was cautiously optimistic. Though if this one didn't work out, there was still one more I was going to see. The house was painted a soft gray color with a white picket fence surrounding the property. There was a garage in the back with a car parked in front of it. The yard was well maintained and looked like there was a small garden off to one side. I wondered if the Jay guy, the owner of the place, did the gardening himself or if he hired someone to do it. I liked the thought that he took pride in the place, including the garden. The street was relatively quiet for a Tuesday evening. I would have expected to see people walking the streets with their dogs or kids to be running around. It still had a pleasant, homey feel even if no one was out. I heard a few dogs barking down the street as I walked up to the front door.

"Coming!" called a voice from behind the door as soon as I knocked.

I waited nervously for him to open the door. It still festered in the back of my mind that I knew him somehow, but I couldn't for the life of me figure out where. Madison was convinced he was some long lost love from when I was younger. But she always was a hopeless romantic.

"Hello, you must be Willow," the man said as he answered the door. His profile picture didn't do him justice. The picture had shown a decent looking man with brown hair and green eyes. What stood before me was so much more. His hair wasn't brown, but sandy as if he had spent a lot of time in the sun. His green eyes were bright and full of mischief as he looked at me. I tried not to stare at him, but it was hard with his broad shoulders and chest. He was taller than I would have thought, standing over six feet. The feeling that I knew him only increased when I saw him, as well as the instant attraction.

"Yes, you must be Jay," I said. Impressed with myself when I didn't stutter.

"Come on in," he said and stepped aside so that I could.

I walked into the foyer and towards what I thought was the living room. It turned out to be more of a great room with an open floor plan. The living room flowed into the kitchen which flowed to the backyard. There were plenty of windows that allow natural light to come in and giving the place a fresh yet relaxed feel. Where I had wondered how much space there was from the outside, I was pleasantly surprised at how big and open it felt.

"Wow, this is impressive," I said.

"Thank you. I just remodeled. I uh, inherited the place from my grandmother when she died," he said.

"Oh, I'm so sorry," I said immediately.

"Thank you. She was ninety-two and had one hell of a life. She loved this place, but it certainly needed some upgrades. Which were a bit more expensive than I would have thought."

"Which is why you're looking for a roommate?" I finished for him.

"Yes. You get it."

"It's not easy making ends meet. I just got offered a job as a paralegal downtown. I would have loved to have found a place on my own but," I said.

"Well, hopefully, our mutual difficulties will be our gains," he said.

I liked his optimism and his smile. He had a way about him that put me at ease. I had been a bit skeptical about living with a guy, but I could easily imagine myself do just that with him. I followed him down the hallway and to the bedrooms.

"My room is just down that way," he said, pointing to the end of the hallway. "But if you like it, this could be your room."

I walked into the room and was pleased to see it was exactly like it looked in the pictures. There was a large queen size bed in the middle of the room that was right below the middle of the large window. There was a chest of drawers and matching desk off to one side, with the closet along with the other. The room was bigger than I had thought and I wondered if it would be big enough for me to fit a small chair in the corner so I could sit and read or write as I wanted.

"This is lovely," I said.

"Thank you. The closet isn't much, but it's an old house, but there's plenty of storage space in the hallway that you would be welcome to use."

"Oh, okay," I said.

"Down the hallway is the bathroom," he said and took me there. It wasn't much, just a long countertop with a toilet at one end and the tub/shower along the opposite wall.

"It's the only one in the house so we would have to share, but as you can see, I'm not too messy. I'm sure we could work out a schedule," he said.

I nodded and then followed him back into the living room.

"Can I get you some water? A soda or something?" he asked as he sat down on the couch.

"No. I'm good. Thank you for asking."

"So, when does the new job start?" he asked.

"Next week. I needed to give notice at my other place and wanted a week to try and get settled if possible," I said.

"Well, that's nice of them. Who are you working for? If you don't mind me asking."

"Smith, Hargrove, and Associates," I said.

"Ah," he said.

"You have never heard of them," I said with a laugh.

"No. But isn't that a good thing. I would be worried if my potential landlord knew all the lawyers in the area."

"Well, unless he was a lawyer," I countered.

"That I am not," he said.

"So, what do you do?" I asked.

"I'm a screenwriter," he said.

"Really," I said.

"Yes, and I actually do decently well with it," he said.

"Do you have any work that I would know?"

"I did a few scary B movies and some made-for-TV movies."

"It's work. Do you like doing it?"

"I love it. I can't imagine doing anything else. I'm working on an original screenplay right now and hope to have the first draft done soon."

"Congrats," I said.

"Thanks," he said.

I stared straight ahead, trying not to look at him and how I couldn't get the feeling that I knew him from somewhere to leave. An awkward silence fell between us and the ease that we had with each other only moments before vanished.

"Please, don't take this the wrong way, but do I know you from somewhere?" he asked.

"You too? I swear I do, but I can't figure it out,"

"What's your last name?" he asked.

"Murphy. And yours?" I asked.

"Stewart," he replied.

It was then that it hit me. "Seriously. Jay Stewart?" I almost yelled at him.

"Wait, you're Willow. Little Willow?" he asked.

It was then that I realized we figured out how we knew each other at the same time. What felt like a lifetime ago, our parents had been married. My mother had met his father on a dating site and within about six months, they had been married. Though my mother had refused to move me out of the school I was in so she and I stayed in our house while Jay and his father, Mark, had stayed in theirs. It had made for an interesting marriage. One that had not lasted more than a few years.

Jay and I only saw each other on the weekends and holidays, but that was about it. It wasn't like we really grew up together, and why it was so easy for us to forget what the other looked like. I do remember him being cute when I was younger. Being three years older than me, he always seemed to have this way about him that was more mature than me. And I had a little bit of a crush on him too. Not that he ever knew or I did anything about it. Luckily, we didn't spend that much time together so I could never be embarrassed by my feelings. By the time I was in high school, our parents had divorced and I had hardly thought about Jay since.

"Wow, you've grown up," he said.

"So, have you," I said and tried not to blush.

"Of all the people to come and try and rent out a room," he said and shook his head.

"Small world," I replied.

"It is. How's your mom?"

"She's good. Single, and happy about it, I think. We don't talk very much. She actually got big into social media and is considered an influencer now. And your dad?"

"Still single. Twice was enough for him. He vowed never to get married again. Still working for the pharmaceutical company," Jay said.

I could almost understand that, the divorce should have been easy, there was hardly any community property between them, but Mom had been bitter for some reason, even though she wanted the divorce. It had dragged on for longer than it should have.

"That sucks," I said.

"He's dated and been happy with that. We all make choices. Speaking of choices. I feel like fate has brought us together again. I would be a fool to offer the room to anyone but you. That is assuming you're interested in taking it," he said.

I was taken back. I hadn't thought he would want me to stay after knowing who I was. I thought it would be too awkward, that we had too much history and it wasn't like our parents had ended on friendly terms. I wasn't sure how smart it would be for me to say yes. Or how it would be if either of our parents wanted to come over.

"Is that a good idea?" I asked.

"Why wouldn't it be? It isn't like we don't know each other. Plus, it won't feel like a stranger is moving in or that you're moving into a stranger's house."

He did have a point, but it wasn't like I knew him that well. We had hardly spent any time together when our parents were married. I had changed since then and he most certainly had. And there was the fact that he was extremely good looking, I had a crush on him when I was younger, it wouldn't do to have those feelings return when we were roommates.

"Look. LA can be a bit scary. This neighborhood is great. There are a few wonderful restaurants and bars all within walking distance. I can show you around, get the lay of the land. Help you get settled. Plus, it would make me feel better knowing that I'm there to keep an eye on you," he said.

"What makes you think I need to be kept an eye on?" I asked.

"Like I said, LA can be scary."

He was making some very valid points and I could feel my resolve slipping. I was half of a mind to see what the other place looked like, but it was farther away from my job and I knew what I was getting with Jay. He seemed friendly enough, and it was kind of nice that we knew each other. What harm would there be in living with him?

"Do you need me to fill out an application or anything like that?" I asked.

"You're family or you were family, so no. Just a handshake will do for now. I might want to draw up a lease with all the legal stuff. I'm sure you would want that for yourself," he said.

He was right, I did.

"I guess in that case, when can I move in?" I asked.

"Whenever you want. The place is yours," he said and beamed at me.

I smiled back but my heart jumped into my throat as he smiled at me. It was one sexy smile and even though I was happy to be moving in with him, I wondered just what had I gotten myself into.

Chapter 2

Jay

"Give me a call if you need anything," I said to Willow as she got in her car.

"Thanks! I will," she said and then drove off.

I watched her go until she was out of sight, then went back into the house. I still couldn't believe that the woman who had been in my house was the same one from my childhood. She had always been a looker. There was something about her even when we were younger that just drew me to her. Her shy smile, her expressive eyes, and how she would look at me that just got to me. I had looked forward to the weekends I spent with my father because it meant I would be seeing her. But when our parents had divorced, we had lost touch. Though after the way her mother treated my father, I didn't blame him.

When Willow had shown up at my door, there was something familiar about her. I kept trying to decide where I knew her, but she hadn't seemed to feel the same way. I knew it wasn't in school or from work and it was only when she said her last name that it clicked. She still looked the same, in some ways, but in others, she had only gotten better looking. She had matured, filled out in all the right places. It had shocked me how attracted I was to her.

At first, I thought I shouldn't offer her the room. There were a few guys I had talked to who seemed promising, and in the back of my mind, I thought it would be better to live with a dude than some chick. But when I started thinking about what it would be like for her if she went and lived with some other guy, and it didn't sit well with me. She was so young and naïve. She might have matured, but she had never lived in the big city. My protective instincts kicked in and I knew I wanted to keep her safe. The only way to do that was to have her stay with me. That way I could keep an eye on her, I could make sure she didn't get into any trouble. It had nothing to do with the fact that I didn't want to think about her staying with some other guy. Who wouldn't be as kind to her, who might take advantage of her.

Though I had immediately thought of doing the same thing. I would be lying if I said that before I knew who she was I had imagined what it would be like if she were in my bed. If we were to make out on my couch. If I were to come up to her while she was in the shower and have my way with her. But those were feelings that I shouldn't be having. She had practically been my sister. We had grown up together. She had agreed to live with me I'm sure as much because of our history and she trusted me. It wouldn't do at all for me to break that trust. If I tried to put a move on her. I would be doing the exact thing I didn't want to happen to her.

The personal chastising did not make my feelings go away.

There was a knock on my back door and then it was immediately opened. I didn't need to look to see that it was my neighbor, Charlie, coming over. Charlie was an out of work actor who had done decently when he was younger, but in recent years hadn't had much success. He lived off the money and investments of his earlier career, so much so that he never had to work. That didn't stop him from coming by, bugging me, and drinking my beer every chance he got.

"So, did you find a hot roommate yet?" he asked as he walked into the living room. He had a beer in his hand and was kind enough to bring one for me.

"I found a roommate, yes," I said as I took the beer.

"Is she smoking hot?" he asked.

My mind immediately flashed on Willow and her smile. There must have been something in my expression because Charlie pointed his finger at me and said, "Oh yeah, she's smoking hot."

"She's my stepsister," I said, a bit more forcefully than I should have.

"Dude! I didn't know your dad was married."

"He isn't," I muttered.

"Wha?" he asked, clearly confused.

"Our parents were married, when we were younger," I stated.

"Ah, so she's still fair game. Excellent," he said.

"Don't even think about it," I said.

"What? Think about what?" he asked all innocently.

"You will not be dating my stepsister or any other roommate I have. Is that clear?" I asked.

"Dude, what's your problem?"

"Willow's going to be living here and she should be treated with the respect that she deserves."

"I respect the hell out of women. No one respects women more than I do. Especially when they're in my bed," he said and lifted his beer in a mock salute.

"Yes, I'm sure that's what all the women in your bed would say. Oh wait, there hasn't been one in there in years," I teased him.

"Dude. That isn't cool," he said.

"Only because it's the truth," I said.

"What about you, man? I saw more women come into your house today than I have in the last six months."

Charlie was right. I had been in a bit of a rut. I had been concentrating so much on writing my screenplay that I had neglected any social engagements, including going out or being with any women. Maybe that was why I had been attracted to Willow; I had been so hard up on not being around women I was just attracted to the first woman I saw. Though as soon as I thought it, I knew that was not the case. There had always been something about Willow and that hadn't changed over time. Seeing her again, all grown up only made it more so.

"Either way. It doesn't matter. I told her she would be safe here. That she would be comfortable. I don't need my weird neighbor coming over and trying to hit on her."

"I wouldn't do that," he said.

In response, I just glared at him. "Well, I might. I can't help it if women find me irresistible," he said.

"That may not be the word I heard to describe you," I answered.

"What have you heard then? Deviously handsome? Charismatic? Sex on a stick?"

"Sex on a stick? Where did you hear such a phrase?" I asked.

"I'm sure I read in a magazine somewhere."

"More like in a cheesy romance novel."

"There's a lot that you can learn from those cheesy romance novels as you like to call them," he said.

"I'll take your word for it," I said.

"Maybe that's what you need to write. A nice romantic comedy," he suggested.

"My screenplay is going just fine, thank you."

"Done with the first draft yet? You gonna let me read it?"

"Almost, and not gonna happen," I said.

"Why not?" he asked and pouted into the beer.

"Because you'll just tell me all the things you hate about it, make me second guess myself, and I'll never get through the second draft."

"That's not," he started and then stopped. "Yeah, I would totally do that."

"So, just leave it alone. And Willow. You got me?" I asked.

"Sure. Sure. I got ya," he said, but he said it half-heartedly and made me wonder if he was really meant it.

"Good. You feel like pizza for dinner?" I asked.

"Yeah. I could do with some pie," he answered.

"Great. Then you can order it and pay for it," I said, and slapped him on the thigh as I went to get us more beer. As I walked back into the kitchen, I wondered how well I would be able to keep my own hands away from the sexy Willow Murphy.

Chapter 3

Willow

"If you could put those boxes in the second bedroom," I said to the movers

It was late in the morning on Saturday and I had just gotten to Jay's, now my house, to unload all my stuff. I had thought that I could move everything on my own, but Madison had told me to suck it up and hire some movers. The day had gone seamlessly for the most part. I felt more energized about unpacking and getting myself settled than if I had to have moved everything myself. It just reminded me that Madison was usually right. I think she also felt guilty that she couldn't help me move as she had to work.

Saying good-bye to her had been hard, and I was glad that we were able to spend Friday together. We had done all our favorite things and stayed up way too late. It was worth it as I wasn't sure when I was going to see her again. Her work schedule was crazy and the drive to see each other was a long one.

"Sure thing," the man said holding a wardrobe box full of my dresses.

"Hey, hey!" Jay said as he walked up to me.

"Hey, yourself. Are you ready for this?" I asked and looked around at the boxes that were scattered around his front yard.

"Very much so," he said and smiled at me. It was the same smile he had given me as we had talked and finalized my moving in. It was the same smile that had haunted my dreams the last week. It was the same smile that I would need to be careful with or I was going to lose my head.

"I know it looks like a lot, but it really isn't that much," I said.

"No worries. We'll find room for it. Do you need any help?" he asked.

"I think the guys have it. I'm gonna go and make sure that they're putting things in the right place," I said and walked away.

"Cool," he said and waved at me.

I waved back as I walked into the house, still a bit surprised that I was going to be living there. That I had made the plunge, not only in starting a new job but with moving in with someone. It felt easier that I knew Jay, he was familiar and yet he wasn't. Which was going to make me feel better and happier about being in a strange place. As long as I could keep my feelings and crush that had resurfaced in check. He had gotten sexier since we were kids, and a bit more laid back. I remember him being a solemn child who didn't talk to me or anyone much. It was good to see that he had mellowed out. It also made him even more attractive, if that was possible.

The next two hours went by quickly as I instructed the movers where to put everything. The two men were very quick and soon everything was out of the van and in either the living room or my bedroom. It still left a bit of a mess for me to clean up and organize, but I was excited about doing it. The chance to unpack my things, put them where I wanted to, it made me feel like this new adventure I was starting on was that much more real.

For the most part, Jay left me alone. He would occasionally come in and check on me. See if I needed anything and even had a conversation or two with the movers. He didn't hover, but he was always just off to the side, like he was keeping an eye on me. Making sure that everything with the movers was on the up and up. It was sweet and something that had never happened to me.

When the movers were gone, I didn't see Jay until later when I came out to start putting my stuff away in the kitchen. I had gotten to a good stopping point in the bedroom and wanted to get started on my kitchen stuff. I also didn't want to keep my boxes lying in the middle of the living room. When I walked into the kitchen, it was to see Jay putting the stuff way. That would have been enough to stop me in my tracks, but the fact that he wasn't wearing a shirt made it even more impressive. He back was to me, which I took as a small blessing, as he hadn't seen me staring at him. I had thought he would be built, toned and muscular, but it was even more evident when he wasn't wearing a shirt. His back muscles were ripped in just the right way, showing that he worked out, but not so much that he was vain about it. His torso didn't seem to have an ounce of fat on it and I found my eyes drawn to his narrow waist and firm ass, which I could still easily make out even in the gym shorts.

I have no idea how long I stood there just staring at his ass, but eventually, I snapped myself out of the trance and walked towards him.

"You didn't have to do that," I said.

"I don't mind helping out," he said as he turned to me.

If I thought the view of his back was amazing, it was nothing compared to seeing his bulging biceps, chiseled chest, and rock-hard six-pack abs. It took everything in me to not reach my hands up and touch him. He was without a doubt the finest looking man I had ever seen. I had to remind myself to breathe, to not stare and to look like it was the most normal thing in the world to see him standing in our kitchen half naked. I wondered if it was a normal occurrence and I was equally excited and petrified by the idea.

"Thanks, that was kind of you," I said.

"You looked like you had your hands full so I thought I could help you in here," he said and put the last cup away.

"I meant to ask you if I even needed to bring any dishes or anything. I assumed you had your own. But I wasn't sure if you would want to share."

"Either way. It's nice to have your own stuff as well. Makes the place feel more like home."

"It is a very nice and homey place," I said and looked around.

"I'm glad you like it and I do hope you feel comfortable here," he said.

"That shouldn't be a problem. Well, since it looks like you have all my kitchen stuff organized, I might enjoy the backyard for a little bit. Take a break."

"Would you like some company?" he asked.

"Yeah, if you want. I figured with it being a Saturday you would have plans," I admitted.

"No. I kept my schedule clear. I wasn't sure if you would need any help."

"Did your dad teach you to be this chivalrous or do you come by it naturally?" I didn't remember his father being this way and was curious where it had come from.

Jay laughed. "No. I will agree with you, Dad is not the most gentlemanly of sorts. I just feel that women need to be treated with respect and you were moving into my place. The lest I could do was hang around in case you had any questions or problems."

"Luckily, that didn't happen. But if you have somewhere else you need to be," I said.

"Are you trying to kick me out of my own house?" he teased.

"No, not at all. I just don't want you to feel obligated to stick around."

"Believe me, it isn't an obligation at all. I want to."

"Okay then," I said, and could feel myself blushing.

"Do you want a beer?" he asked.

"Sure," I said. I hadn't had a chance to go to the store and that was on my list of things to do but I had needed a small break. I hadn't thought it would turn into having a drink with my new and very sexy roommate

The backyard wasn't huge, but Jay had used the space wisely. There was a small patio right outside the back door that held a table and four chairs. There was a large square patch of grass with a smattering of trees around it, which helped to offer some shade to the house and yard. Off in the corner, there was a small firepit with four Adirondack chairs surrounding it.

"How often do you use the firepit?" I asked when we were both seated at the table.

"Not as often as I would like or should," he said.

"Work keep you busy?" I asked and took a sip of the beer.

"It can. There's usually a lull and then it gets really crazy. It isn't stable. It's never easy and more than likely I will get a screenplay rejected more than I will get it accepted. But I wouldn't trade it for anything else in the world."

"That's wonderful."

"What about you? Are you excited about starting the new job?"

"I think so."

"What does that mean?" he asked and leaned a little bit closer to me.

It took me a moment to respond. Suddenly, he felt too close, his masculine smell filled my nostrils, his green eyes filled my vision. I could feel my heart rate increasing at just having him that close to me. I leaned back in my chair, trying to give myself some space and some time to form a coherent thought.

"It's a bit scary. It's a pretty big law firm and I just hope that I do well," I stated.

"I'm sure you'll do fine. You were always so smart. They're lucky to have you."

"How do you know I'm smart?" I asked.

"Come on. I remember how smart you were when we were younger. I can't imagine that's changed."

I was shocked that he remembered anything about me, much less that I had been a bit of a bookworm when I was younger.

"No, it hasn't. I'm still a bit of a nerd," I said and quickly took a drink of my beer.

"Well, there's nothing wrong with being a nerd. I think nerds are sexy," he said.

"Spoken like a man who isn't nerdy at all," I said.

"Really? You don't think I'm a nerd? I sit in front of a computer all day and try and write stories. That can be pretty nerdy."\

"You write screenplays that get turned into television shows or movies. That's not nerdy at all."

"Maybe. I wish it were more glamorous. But most people don't even give the writer the time of day, much less any acknowledgments."

"Are you okay with that?" I asked.

"It's the nature of the job. If I didn't want it, I shouldn't do it. Right?" he asked and finished the last of his beer. "Do you want another one?" he asked and eyed my beer.

I had drunk it faster than I usually did as much because I was nervous

"No. I shouldn't. I actually should see about getting to the store. Stocking up and figuring out dinner."

"Do you want to get a pizza? There's a great place near here that delivers," he offered.

"Um. I really want to get settled," I said.

"Oh. Yeah. I get it. Totally," he said, but I could tell he was a bit disappointed by my comment.

It had been nice to sit and talk to him. I could have easily spent the rest of the night doing just that. It wouldn't be difficult at all to imagine that we would do it every night. That we were friends, that we could even be something more. My attraction to him had only gotten more intense in the small bit of time that we had hung out. I could see it only getting worse. The sooner I established the boundaries that we were roommates and nothing more, the better off I would be.

He was just being nice; he was just making sure that I was settled in and comfortable. There was no way that he would be interested in me. I knew that, even as my heart longed for it to be different. I couldn't let my silly crush get in the way of us having a mutually respectful relationship as roommates. Nothing more. Which included not having another beer and some pizza with him.

"Maybe some other time," I said as I got up.

"I'd like that," he said.

"Have a good night. Thanks for the beer," I said and walked back into the house.

Before I turned down the hallway, I looked back to see Jay sitting there staring off into space.

Chapter 4

Jay

I sat and looked out onto the backyard long after Willow had left. I hadn't lied to her when I said that I had cleared my day so that I could be around for her. What I didn't tell her was the real reason was because I wanted to see her again. That I had been excited about having her move in. To being able to look at her and talk to her again. She had been on my mind a lot the last few days. More so than any other woman in a very long time. I lived and worked in Los Angeles, it wasn't like there was a shortage of beautiful and willing women for me to find. But I had been completely uninterested in them since I had gotten back in touch with Willow. With the screenplay being close to completion, I should have been thinking about getting back into my social life. Seeing some friends and women that I hadn't seen in a while, but I didn't care about any of that. All I cared about was Willow and seeing her.

She had said she had a chair, a lot of clothes and books that she wanted to move so she had wanted to use a moving company. I had originally offered to help her move the stuff, seeing if I could borrow a friend's truck. But she had refused, stating she wanted to do it herself. On the one hand, I could admire her need for independence, but it also frustrates me that she didn't want me to help her out. I was used to women wanting it, even asking for it before I even could offer it. It only reminded me that Willow wasn't like any other woman I knew.

Case in point, she hadn't wanted any help with the move or with getting things organized. I had hung around when she and the movers showed up thinking for sure she would need me then, but she hadn't. It had taken everything in me to not constantly go and check on her, to see if I could help her. Even just be around her. Of course, she didn't need anything and I was afraid I was starting to see a pattern forming. One that I didn't like. It was almost out of sear boredom and frustration that I had started to put her kitchen stuff away. It was nice to actually look and see what she had. I felt like I was getting to know her better when I saw what type of dishes she had. What cups she had chosen. Most of them were a strange mix making me think that she had gotten them used or from a thrift store. It only made me admire her need to make every dollar count.

I knew what it was like to start fresh, to have to save everything you made. That even going out to eat was a treat. Which was why I had offered to buy us some pizza. I had thought it would be a good way for us to get to know each other better. We had been having such a pleasant conversation over the beers, I didn't see what harm there would be in continuing it with dinner and more drinks. I had even thought about seeing if she wanted to go and check out the local bars later in the night. I wanted to show her the area, make sure she felt comfortable walking around. There were many great places to go, and I wanted to show them to her. I wanted to see her excitement at the new places, to be the one who showed them to her. To have that connection with her.

In my mind, I tried to convince myself it was because I wanted her to be happy in our house. For her to feel that it was hers, as well as mine. I wanted her to want to go out and have fun. That it could be hard to find new places that you felt comfortable going to. I had been there and understood it. But it was more than that. I wanted to spend more time with her. I wanted to hang out with her, talk to her, look at her, just be around her. I tried not to be too offended when it was evident that she didn't feel the same way.

Just because I felt like there was something there between us. Just because I thought I had seen her looking at my chest when we were in the kitchen. Just because I had felt a bit of chemistry between the two of us. Just because I had imagined what it would be like to pull her into my arms and kiss her. It didn't mean she felt the same way.

I had wanted her to be my roommate because we knew each other, because I felt a need to watch out for her. If it had grown into feelings and she didn't feel the same way, that was on me to deal with not her. She was still new in town and I needed to help her get settled. I would need to find a way to put my own feelings and lust aside to do that. She was starting a new job, she was in a new environment, she needed a friend, a confidant, not some man trying to get into her pants. I needed to remember that and respect that. I needed to find a way to be what she wanted me to be, not what I wished to be.

Thinking and doing it were two very different things. When she left to go to the store, I had grabbed some leftover food and taken it into my room. I told myself it was because I wanted to give her space, to not make her think that I was hovering when she came back. It was as much that but also that I felt it was best if I didn't see her again that night. That I needed to get my mind in the right place. She was my ex-stepsister, we were roommates, and I would need to think of her that way, not as some woman I wanted to bed.

I spent the night binge watching a drama and trying my best to not think and wonder about Willow and what she was doing. I had been doing a good job until she went into the bathroom and took a shower. My mind immediately started thinking about her taking off her shorts and T-shirt. Of her stepping into the shower and letting the warm water hit her body. My body responded to the image of her lathering up a washcloth and running her hands all over her body. I could imagine her nipples getting hard as she rubbed the soap over them. Was she the type of woman who pleasured herself in the shower? I liked to think that she was and what it would be like if I were to join her in the shower. If I could run my hands along her breasts. If I could be the one that brought them to rock hard peaks. That I could be the one to slip my fingers inside her, to play with her clit and listen to her as she moaned out my name. To feel her body surround me as I entered her and took her over and over again.

The images stayed in my mind, long after she had left the shower. I knew it was wrong to think of her that way. She had come here because she trusted me, she needed me to look out for her. I couldn't dishonor that trust by doing precisely what I had been trying to save her from. No matter how sexy she looked, no matter how much I longed to take her into my arms, I knew I could never do that. We were to be roommates, friends if I was lucky, and that was all. Any feelings, any hopes that I had that we would be something more would have to be pushed aside. I couldn't do that; I wouldn't do that to her.

I would have to find a way to suppress my feelings for her. My longing to have her as mine, and there was a need, so overwhelming that it shocked me. I had never felt so strongly about a woman the way I did about Willow. But they were only my feelings, my thoughts and I would have to curb them and my reaction to her. As I went to bed that night, I had no idea how I was going to do that or if I was even going to be able to stop my growing feelings for Willow.

Chapter 5

Willow

When I woke up the next morning, I was still tired and a bit stiff. I had tossed and turned all night long. I thought it was because I was in a new place, in a new bed, and it was unfamiliar, but I knew it was because of Jay and how I had been with him the night before. He had only been trying to be nice to me, to make me feel welcome and I had shot him down. It wasn't his fault that I thought he was sexy, that I was starting to have a feeling for him that I knew he would never have for me. I hadn't handled the situation right and had treated him unfairly. I knew I had offended him, so much so that he had gone into his room and not come out the rest of the night. I had felt bad about that and as I had gone to sleep, I kept thinking about ways that I could make it up to him.

We were going to be living together, seeing each other daily. I was sure at some point he would bring a woman home with him. I was going to have to find a way to be around him and not let my hormones go into overdrive. To be okay seeing him with another woman and taking her into his bed. As I got up and walked out of my room, I vowed it was a new day, and it was a new chance for me to make nice with him. To have the type of relationship I should have with my roommate. With a newfound purpose, I walked into the kitchen to see him making breakfast. He was dressed in a long sleeve shirt and gym shorts. I told myself to ignore how good he looked in them. How easy it was to see his muscles through the shirt.

"Do you live here?" I asked.

"Um, why yes. Yes, I do," he said.

I blushed and then walked over to get a coffee cup. "I mean do you live in the kitchen. It seems every time I see you, you're in here."

"It's a nice kitchen. But no. I think you've just gotten lucky. I was about to make some eggs; do you want some?" he asked.

It was on the tip of my tongue to tell him no, that he didn't need to put himself out like that, but I refrained. He was trying to be helpful, he wanted to make me breakfast. It was a nice thing that a roommate would do, so I should let him.

"That would be lovely," I said and went to make myself some tea.

"Not a coffee drinker?" he asked as he turned to me holding his own cup.

"Never got into it. I take it you like coffee?" I asked.

"Yes. I can't live without it. I'm actually a morning person, but I still like to have my cup of joe to get things started. How do you like your eggs?" he asked and turned back to the stove.

"Scrambled would be great. Can I make some toast or something?" I asked.

"There's some fruit in the fridge. It should hopefully still be good. I was actually going to see if you wanted to head to the Farmer's Market with me, pick up some fresh fruit and vegetables from the area. Maybe get a lay of the land."

I had planned on spending the day in my room, making sure everything was organized and seeing if I needed to get anything, but the idea of spending the day with him, with getting us on even footing and maybe even as friends, seemed like a much better idea. "That sounds like fun," I said.

Jay turned around and beamed at me. His smile going all the way to his eyes and causing my heart to leap into my throat. I swallowed slowly and concentrated on getting my heart rate and breathing to go back to normal. We were going to friends, that was all, I said to myself over and over.

"It's an outstanding market. They don't just have fresh produce, but they have a lot of other cool stuff, even some old books and jewelry. It's fun to just wander around. Usually there are some food trucks hanging around and sometimes there's even some music," he said. His back was to me as he finished cooking the eggs.

I busied myself getting the fruit out and cutting them up.

"Did you sleep okay last night?" he asked.

"Yes, like a baby. The bed is very comfortable," I said. The bed was indeed comfortable, but I wasn't about to tell him that I hadn't slept well because I had been thinking about him all night.

"I'm glad you liked it," he said.

We chatted easily as we finished making breakfast. He poured himself some coffee and I brought over some orange juice for myself. The eggs were fluffy and delicious and I told him so.

"Thanks. I put a little sour cream in them, it helps," he said.

"I never would have thought that," I replied as I took another large helping of the eggs. "How long have you lived here?"

"Ah, about a year. I was renting a really crappy apartment before then and was happy to be able to move into this place."

"It really is a great place. I can't wait to check out the area."

"I think you'll like it. The people are really friendly and most stuff is within a few minutes' walk from here."

"That's wonderful. I was hoping to find something like that. Local shops and restaurants or even a bar or two. I would even love it if I could do my grocery shopping and not use a car, though that may not work."

"The deli down the way is actually decently priced. But otherwise, Sally's around the corner is the best."

"You certainly know your way around the area," I said and got up and went to the sink. When I turned on the water and started washing my dishes, Jay got up and stood next to me.

"What are you doing?" he asked. As he spoke, I felt his breath on my neck, sending shivers down my spine. I dropped the dish I was holding and it took all my willpower to keep my knees from buckling. I could sense his hands inches from my waist and I ached to have him touch me, to turn me around, and kiss me. But I knew he wasn't going to do that so I took a deep breath and said. "The dishes. What does it look like?"

"You don't have to do that," he countered.

I turned around to look at him and as soon as I did, I realized it was a mistake. He was too close, it was like he was invading my very space just like he had invaded my almost every waking thought since I met him. His eyes were big and expressive as he looked at me. I watched transfixed as his eyes darted from my eyes and to my lips and back up again.

"We have a dishwasher for that," he said and reached across to take a dish out of the sink.

I watched him as he went next to the sink and put the dish in the dishwasher. It took me a minute to move, to think, to realize that I must look like a fool standing there staring at him with my mouth wide open. "You use it?" I asked.

"Of course, I use it. Why wouldn't I?"

"Mom had one and never did. She said it didn't get the dishes clean enough. And then I never had one in any other place to be able to," I said.

"Definitely use it. I do and if you don't, I'll feel bad," he said.

He had moved away from me so I could think a little bit better. "We should discuss chores and all that at some point," I said.

"Clean up after yourself; otherwise, I have a cleaning woman that comes in once a week on Thursdays."

"Really?" I asked. The thought of not having to vacuum, clean the bathroom, or dust had a fantastic appeal.

"Yes. It's one thing that I really splurge on."

"Do I need to help pay for it?" I asked and went to get the rest of the dishes to put them in the dishwasher.

"No. Not at all. It's part of the price you pay for the room."

"Alright. Cool." I said.

Jay closed the dishwasher and smiled at me. "How soon do you want to head to the Farmer's Market?" he asked.

"Can you give me like twenty minutes?" I asked.

"Sure. I'll need more than that. Shall we say about half an hour?" he asked.

"Okay," I said and watched him head to his bedroom.

I took a few minutes before heading back to my room to compose my thoughts and clean the counters. It had been nice to hang out with Jay to talk and catch up a little bit. It was so easy to talk to him and to be around him. I wanted to have more of that, to be able to be comfortable with him and hopefully start a friendship that would last for many years. There were still my lingering feelings for him, and how I overreacted to them, yet again. I couldn't believe what a fool I had been to think that he wanted to kiss me. That he could be interested in me when all he was doing was being kind. That was all he had been since the moment he had opened up the door. It wasn't right for me to think or hope that there could be something more between us.

Just because I had longed to have him kiss me. Just because I thought he was going to or that he had a look in his eyes that said he did for the briefest of moments, didn't mean that it was actually there. I was being unrealistic about how he saw me, what he wanted from me. He saw me as a little sister, someone he needs to look out for. Nothing more. He was taking the day to show me around the area, to make sure I knew where to go and what to do. That if nothing else should prove to me that he was only being a good roommate and ex-stepbrother.

The sooner he felt I knew the lay of the land the sooner he could do his own thing and not have to worry about me. I knew it was only out of a sense of obligation and history that he was even doing any of this. I would be wise to just enjoy the time that I had with him, make sure we were friendly to each other so that we could live together peacefully. The last thing I needed to do was make my feelings for him known and then cause awkwardness between us.

I had just moved in. I wanted to stay. I liked the house; I liked the area. It was the perfect location for me and work. I shouldn't do anything stupid to jeopardize any of that. Soon enough he would be bringing women back to the house or staying with them. He was too good looking to stay single or without a woman in his bed for long. I needed to find a way to get over what I was feeling and to enjoy the opportunity I had. Not only in the place that I was staying but also with the man I got to share it with.

It was a second chance to know a man who had been my brother for a few years. It might be fun to talk about our parents, to remanence about our childhoods. I had always wanted siblings, but the closest I ever go to it was with Jay. If I played my cards right, we could be friends, even good friends and I would be lucky to have that. Any infatuation I had in my head was just that, in my head.

With the kitchen counter cleaned, I headed to my bedroom, determined to make the best of the day with Jay and to solidify our friendship and just friendship once and for all.

Chapter 6

Jay

The day had been wonderful. I had always liked going to the Farmer's Market and on the rare occasion that there was a woman in my bed on Sunday morning, I would take her. It was nice to have a woman on my arm as I strolled by the different booths. Chatting with the vendors, enjoying the day and talking with some of the patrons that I had gotten to know through the small bit of time I had lived in the area. Yet, somehow it was so much better when I was with Willow.

It was as if she had never been to a Farmers Market before. She marveled at all the sites, the booths, the food, the people, everything. It was hard to keep up with her as she kept walking quickly from one booth to the other as if she was afraid to miss anything. Her excitement was contagious and the vendors were all happy to give her samples or talk to her about their products. Every booth she went to, she wanted to buy something and eventually, she came up to me and told me she had to stop or she would buy out the entire market.

At that moment, I didn't see anything wrong with it and almost suggested she do just that. Instead, we went and sat in the grass with some ice cream and listened to the band play. She didn't sit still for very long but soon started dancing around. Her hands twirling in the air as she moved in time with the music. It was a sight to see. I had never seen anyone so uninhibited as she was. Who didn't care what she looked like or what others thought of her. She got a few looks from other people as they walked by. Los Angeles had its share of strange people and so she wasn't out of the ordinary. But a lot of looks and comments were sweet even favorable towards her.

I wished I could be that free, but I wasn't. I had always been a bit shy and reserved when I was a kid. I made friends slowly and my father moved around a lot so it was hard to keep them for very long. I remember Willow being shy but friendly and was never at a loss of people to hang out with. I had admired it back when we were younger and I could see it had only gotten better the older she had gotten.

Once the band was done playing, we wandered around a little bit more, but Willow insisted that we head back or we would never be able to carry all that she had, and I had to agree. I told her we could come back next weekend and bring more bags to take all our stuff. She happily agreed and squeezed my forearm in excitement. It was the first time she had touched me since we had been in the kitchen.

When I had stood next to her and her soft sweet smell had surrounded me. When she had looked up at me with her wide-eyed innocence and made me want to kiss her. After breakfast I had gone and taken a cold shower, needing the time to cool myself off. Telling myself that I needed to keep my distance, that I shouldn't get that close to her. That I shouldn't tempt myself like that. And I had been good all day, enjoying the time talking to her, making myself think that we would be friends. That everything was going to be okay.

But all it took was her touching me once, in the simplest of ways for my newfound resolve to slip. I smiled at her as I tried to calm my own feelings. And it took all my willpower to continue walking next to her as if nothing had happened. I tried to get my mind off her touching me and asked her what she had been up to since we had seen each other last. She told me about her college days and deciding to become a lawyer and then it not working out and choosing to be a paralegal. I told her about coming to Los Angeles and the fears of not making it and the excitement when I did enough to pay the bills.

"Do you ever think or hope that you will make it really big?" she asked as we walked back into the house.

"It would be nice, but I do not think it will happen," I said.

Why not?" she said and put the food on the counter.

"It's a tough field, it's an even tougher industry. I'm happy with my success. I hope my screenplay does well. If not there's always the pilot season."

She started organizing all the things that she had purchased and I shook my head as I walked up behind her. "Are you gonna be able to eat all of this?".

"I'll find a way. I might be looking up ways to make all of it, but yes," she said and blushed slightly.

It didn't think about how it was the second time she had blushed that day.

"You looked like you were having a good time," I said to her as I started putting the food in the refrigerator.

"I was, the best," she beamed at me.

"I'm glad," I said my head in the refrigerator

"Is that band there every week?" I asked.

"Not always, they usually have someone there, but it isn't always the same group. Did you want to see them again?"

"If possible."

"I can see if I can find them playing anywhere locally. They usually are," I said.

"You don't have to do that," I said.

"It would be fun. What are roommates for?" I asked.

"There is that," she said and looked down.

I got the impression that I had said something wrong. That I had overstepped my boundaries as her roommate. "Unless there's someone else you want to go with?" I asked.

"Oh, no. You're the only person I know around here," she said and then blushed even deeper. "I mean I would love to go to the concert with you."

"I'll see what I can find," I said. "Um, are you hungry? Do you want to think about dinner? Maybe decide what to do with your new loot?"

"I'm not overly hungry, but maybe later. I thought I could make some stir fry. Would you like some?"

When she had first started talking, I thought for sure she was going to tell me she didn't want to eat or spend any more time with me. I was glad to see that wasn't the case.

"That would be nice," I said.

"I'm um, going to go and take a shower and then get some stuff ready for tomorrow. But I'll see you for dinner later."

"That you will," I said and smiled to myself that I was going to be able to spend more time with her.

I had never been with a woman that was so easy to just be with than Willow. The entire day had passed in a blink of an eye. She was so happy and excited about everything that she saw; it was easy for the feelings to flow into me. I was happier than I had been in a long time and I hadn't realized how much I had been staying home. How much I had been avoiding being around people until Willow was around. I had gotten so obsessed with finishing my screenplay that nothing else had mattered. It became very evident by how I was greeted like a lost relative by some of the vendors when we were at the market. I was trying my best to be friendly and courteous with Willow but she was just so sexy it was hard for me not to imagine what it would be like to take her into my arms. To kiss her, to hold her, to throw her over my shoulder and take her into my bedroom.

I had resisted the urge to take her hand as we were walking around the market. I had seen some of the looks from the vendors and I was sure they thought we were together. It was a sentiment that I was not opposed to. I had introduced her as my new roommate and if I got some knowing looks, I didn't discourage them.

As I watched her walk away and thought of spending the evening with her and not kissing her, I knew I wasn't going to be able to handle it. She had to be feeling what I was. That there was something between us. I know we only just got back into each other's lives but there was a chemistry, a connection. I had felt it twice now in the kitchen and once when I touched her at the market. I knew it wasn't right and that I should stop the feelings and thoughts I was having, but I couldn't. I was attracted to her, and I got the impression she was attracted to me. What harm would there be in seeing if I was right? I wasn't going to push too far; just test the waters out so to speak. I didn't want to scare her away if she didn't feel the same way, but I didn't want to waste any time that we could have together if I could.

Or maybe I was just really horny and wanted her.

It was later that the smells coming from the kitchen drew me out. "Wow, that smells amazing," I said as I walked into the kitchen.

Willow didn't turn around as she said, "Thanks. It should be ready in a few minutes. I was about to get you."

"The smells called me in. What all do you have in there?" I asked.

I had stepped next to her and leaned over her shoulder trying to get a better view of what she was cooking. As I did, she tensed up next to me and closed her eyes. I quickly stepped away and went to the refrigerator to get a beer. Maybe I was wrong in thinking she was interested in me.

"Do you want one?" I asked, trying to keep the friendly, comfortable banter we had earlier in the day.

"Please," she said and still didn't turn around.

I tried to not be offended. I put her beer on the counter next to her and went to sit on the kitchen table. "You all ready for tomorrow?" I asked.

"Somewhat. I still have a few things I want to do. Some more research on my bosses and the company."

"That's smart," I said.

"I hope so. I'm not totally sure what to expect when I get there," she said.

"You'll find out tomorrow. Can I help you with anything?" I asked.

"Can you get out some plates?"

"Sure," I said and did as she asked. By the time I had gotten the table set up, she was putting the food on the table. The ease that we had with each other was back, moving around each other as if we had been doing it for years, not less than a few days.

"What is your screenplay about?" she asked when we had started eating.

I spent the rest of the meal talking to her about the screenplay. An epic love story that goes back and forth between modern times and World War II. As I told her about it, she asked questions, wanted to know about the characters, the plot, the setting, everything. She asked insightful questions about the plot points and the character development that I hadn't even thought about.

We talked into the night, having a few more beers as we did. I was enjoying having someone talk to about my screenplay who seemed as excited about it as I was. I had been hesitant to speak to anyone, to show anyone my work before I had anything more concrete, but I felt like I could and I would want to with Willow. After talking to her, I was also needed to do a change a few things before she or anyone else would see it. But I had a renewed vigor about it and confidence that it would do well. That someone would want to buy it.

I marveled at how her eyes would light up when I got excited about one of her suggestions. How she would take the idea and run with it, making it better than her original thought. Before I knew it, it was late in the night and I knew that I should let her go to bed, but I didn't want her to go. I wanted to keep talking to her. The attraction I felt for her only grew the longer I was with her. I wanted to reach out and take her hand, to tug the stray strand of hair behind her ear. Something, anything. But I held off. I still wasn't totally sure how she felt about me and was wary of pushing things when we were doing so well.

"I should let you go to bed," I said.

"It's not that late," she replied and then looked at the clock. "That can't be right!" she said and giggled.

"I hate to say it, but it is. You have a big day tomorrow. You should get some sleep."

"Yes. I should, but this has been so lovely. I've never thought about writing or creating anything before. Thank you for letting me hear all about it."

"I'm the one who should be thanking you for all the ideas."

"They were just my own thoughts. I'm sure you have better ones."

She started cleaning up the last of the beer bottles. I stood up to help her and was standing next to her when she swayed a little bit. I reached out to hold her. The electricity between us was palpable. My hands gripped onto her arms tightly. If it was to keep her upright or to hold onto her for a little longer, I honestly didn't know. Willow's head was down and as she slowly lifted her eyes to look at me, I could feel her shock as her body responded to mine. I knew at that moment, all my thoughts of being good, of keeping my hands to myself had been futile. I was going to kiss her; I was going to wrap my arms around her and push her up against my body. I was going to know what it was like to feel my mouth pressed up against hers. To slide my tongue inside her mouth. To hear her moan as I kissed her. That all my conflicted thoughts were right. She did have feelings for me. She did want to kiss me as much as I her.

"I must be tipsier than I thought," she said and blushed.

It was like a cold bucket of water had been thrown on my body. She wasn't feeling or thinking the same things I was. She was only a bit drunk and I wasn't going to take advantage of that. I wasn't that type of guy.

"That's okay. You should get to bed. I'll clean up in here," I said and helped to steady her and then stepped away. I turned away from her to prevent her from seeing my hard-on.

"Um, Sweet dreams," she said and I heard her quietly walk down the hall. I didn't turn around until after she had closed her door. Not trusting myself to not go and try and take her into my arms. I threw the beers away and put my hands on the counter and leaned my head forward. Trying to calm down my raging emotions and overwhelming feelings. I knew I needed to do something about my feelings for Willow but for the life of me I couldn't figure out what it should be.

Chapter 7

Willow

I am sure it was the alcohol and the late hour that I went to bed that helped me to sleep that night. I woke up rested and ready to start the day. I got dressed with a renewed passion for my job and my new life. I wasn't going to think about Jay and how it had felt to be in his arms last night. I wouldn't think about how he had looked at me, really looked at me as we had talked the night before. I wouldn't think about how at times I felt he was looking at me as something more than his sister. As someone he would want to kiss. I wouldn't think about how stupid I had felt when I thought he was going to kiss me, only to turn away as if he was repulsed by me.

The thought there might be the start of something between us had all been in my head. That he might have been interested in me. But I knew after last night that wasn't the case at all. He wanted to be friends and he was a good friend and roommate. I should be happy with that; I should feel lucky that he was so kind and considerate with me. That he told me about his screenplay and was open to my ideas.

The evening had been going so well, I couldn't believe how it had just passed in a blink of an eye. Jay was someone that I could talk to for hours. That I never tired of hearing his stories, of listening to his voice, of merely looking at him. He had such a passion for his work. I had taken the job as a paralegal as much because I needed a job, I needed a change of scenery and I needed to try something new. My job was just a job but with Jay, the screenplay was something he cared about, deeply, was passionate about, and I admired that.

I had wanted to feel more of that. I wanted to know if he could have that same passion as he held me, kissed me, and made love to me. I had thought for just a moment, for one glorious moment, that he had felt that way. That he wanted to kiss me, but just as soon as it had been there, it was gone. It happened so quickly I was sure that I had imagined it. That was the only explanation I could come up with. And as wonderful as that feeling had been it had hurt so much more when I realized I was wrong. I wasn't going to let myself feel that way again. I wasn't going to put myself through that hurt that heartache.

The weekend had been amazing, and I would have to live with the memories of that. Today, I started a new job and I needed to think about that, about my life now that I was in a new town. It wouldn't help to think about a man I could never have. I would do what I had set out to do when I first thought of doing this. I would go out, explore, see, and have little adventures. I would do what I could to stay away from Jay. To let him live his life and I would live mine.

It didn't surprise me to see him sitting in the kitchen looking at his tablet as he drank of cup of coffee when I walked into the kitchen.

"Good morning," I said as cheerfully as I could.

"Good morning. Ready for your first day?" he asked.

"As ready as I'll ever be."

"Can I make you some breakfast before you go?"

"No. I need to get going, but thank you," I said.

"Oh, okay. Well, good luck. Let me know how it goes. Maybe we could get dinner and celebrate after?" he asked.

There was nothing I wanted more than to celebrate my first day of work with Jay. To sit and tell him about it, but I knew I couldn't do that. I wasn't ready. My feelings were still too fresh, too new, and too evident. I wanted to be friends with him, I wanted to be able to be in the same room with him without wanting to kiss him. I wasn't there yet. I would hopefully be soon. But for now, I needed to stay away, to put some distance between us, and get my feelings under control.

"That would be great, but I think my new boss wanted to take me out. Give a little critique of my day and everything."

"Well, that's nice of them. I hope you have a good time."

"Thanks, I will," I said and walked out the door.

I hated lying to him, but if I had told him that I was going to stick close to work, for the simple fact that I needed to stay away from him, that wouldn't do. I was going to go and see the city, maybe find a nice bar, coffee shop, or restaurant near work that I could hopefully become a local at. If I could get some co-workers or even my boss to go with me even better.

Any thought that I was going to make friends or that my new job was going to rewarding or even fun went out the window as soon as I walked in the door. My boss, Cathy, was waiting for me, and she was pissed.

"You're late," she said.

I looked at my watch and saw that I was actually about ten minutes earlier than I was supposed to be there, but I wasn't going to say anything. Nor was I going to give her an excuse I could tell she didn't want.

"Come on. I haven't got all day," she said and ushered me into the office.

I was given a very quick and brief overview of the office, what the basic layout was and then was ushered to my desk. It was a small cubical surrounded by other cubicles in a room that had no windows. I was quickly told that I needed to look through a mountain of paperwork and it needed to be completed by the end of the day. Looking at it, I thought for sure I wasn't going to get it all done, but I knew that Cathy wouldn't care or want to hear my concerns.

Instead, I plastered a smile on my face that I didn't feel and went to work. I barely left my desk for the rest of the day. There might have been some people around me working but I never lifted my head long enough to talk to them or introduce myself. Though no one came up to speak to me so I didn't think I was being rude. The office was too busy for anyone to be considered rude.

The only time I left my desk was to use the restroom and to grab some lunch. Though I immediately brought it back and ate it at my desk while I continued my work. It was at the very end of the day that I saw Cathy again. She only came by long enough to see what I had accomplished, look at me disapprovingly when I wasn't as far along as she thought I should be and walk away. I was half worried she was going to fire me and I wasn't even sure if I should come back the next day. But I needed the job and as long as she didn't tell me flat out to not come in or that I was fired, I was going to come in.

By the time I walked out of the office, I was too tired to think about doing any exploring, or doing anything else but going back to the house and doing nothing. The day had been so stressful that I didn't even want to eat. I wanted to call Madison and tell her everything that had been going on but she was away on a cruise with her boyfriend and wouldn't be around for a week.

As I took the train back to my house, I thought about Jay. He had texted me a few times during the day, but I had been so busy I hadn't had a chance to write back, except to say that I was working. He had seemed to understand as he didn't text me the rest of the day. The closer I got to home, the more excited I was to see him. Maybe we could still get that dinner that he suggested or maybe that pizza he had been talking about.

I wasn't sure if I was up for going out, but I was up for talking to him. I wanted to tell him about my day, to see what he thought about it and if I should even continue with it. In my mind, I could see him telling me that I should stick it out, that it was only the first day and it was bound to get better. But if it didn't then I could always look for another job. I wanted to hear him tell me that, to say to me that it was going to be okay. I had felt so lonely being at work that it was nice to think that I could go home and see him. To a friendly face.

"Hey, you'll never guess the day I had," I said as I walked in.

I wasn't even sure that Jay was home and when I walked into the living room and saw that only one light was on, I wondered if he was. He hadn't told me if he was going to be around or not, but he didn't need to tell me and I had told him I would be out. I shook my head as I shrugged off my jacket and started to hang it up, only to hear some movement on the couch.

The sound startled me so much that I froze. My eyes shot to the couch to hear what sounded like giggling.

"Hello?" I called.

Slowly, two heads peaked up out from the front of the couch. One I recognized easily as Jay, but the other was a woman I had never seen before. It was evident that I had interrupted them as they were both in various stages of undress.

"Oh. My goodness. Um. I'm so sorry. I didn't realize," I said and tried to make a quick exit out of the room.

"Willow. Wait," Jay called, standing up with his hand out in front of him.

I looked past his hand to his pants and could see the huge tent he was making in them.

"No. It's okay. I should have told you I was coming home. You have company. I'll just get out of your way," I said and practically ran to my bedroom.

I considered it a blessing that I made it to my bedroom before I started crying. Any thoughts, any hopes that I had that Jay might be interested me in flew out the window. Of course, he didn't. Why would he? The woman he had in his living room was gorgeous. She was probably a model or something like that. Why would he be interested in someone like me when he could have someone like that? I rolled myself onto my bed and cried. I cried because I was stressed and tired from the day, from losing all chances of Jay and I being something. For being a fool and moving to a city that I wasn't strong or ready enough to deal with. I couldn't believe the situation I had gotten myself into and had no idea how to get myself out of it.

Chapter 8

Jay

I hadn't expected Willow to come home. I hadn't known what to do when she had and saw Rachel and me together. I had been too shocked and embarrassed by her seeing me there that I had stood in the middle of the living room looking like a fool. I watched as Willow walked into her room and quietly closed the door. The sound of the door closing echoed through the house, reminding what a dupe I had been.

Rachel reached up and ran her hand up my bicep. "Where were we?" she asked and tried to pull me back towards her and the couch.

I resisted her and moved away from her. "You should probably go," I said.

"Why? I don't mind if she's here. I can be quiet if I need to. Or loud," she said and giggled.

Rachel and I had met about six months ago through some mutual friends. She was attractive, fun, and a little adventurous in bed. We had enjoyed ourselves for a few weeks and then it had fizzled. I couldn't remember if I stopped texting her, or if she stopped texting me. Either way, we had lost touch, until a few days ago when she started texting me again. Telling me she missed me, wanted to know what I was up to, and if we could meet up. I knew what she wanted and I hadn't responded to her. I was too involved with getting Willow situated in the house that I didn't have time for Rachel.

But after the weekend I had with Willow, I needed a distraction, I needed to lose myself in another woman. I needed to get my mind off of Willow and I felt the only way was by hanging out with someone else. I thought maybe if I was with Rachel, I wouldn't think about Willow and how sweet she had looked throughout the whole weekend. I wouldn't think about her sleeping in a bed that was on the opposite side of my wall. I wouldn't think about how it would feel if she was in my arms.

It had been working, somewhat. Rachel had come over and we had enjoyed a nice bottle of wine and caught up on each other's lives. We both knew it was just foreplay for the main event and soon we were making out on the couch. I had thought to take things into the bedroom, but she hadn't wanted to. Which was why when Willow had come home, she saw us in a state of half-dressed and me with a raging boner.

I could tell that Willow was shocked by what she had seen. I had told her that I rarely had other people over and within two days of her moving in I had brought a woman home. That wasn't the way to keep a cordial relationship with my roommate. It wasn't the way to show her that I respected her and her space. Any interest that I had in Rachel had left as soon as Willow had walked into the house. I had known it was a mistake as soon as I saw Willow. I never should have invited Rachel over. I wasn't into her, I had only used her to try and get over Willow, and it wasn't going to work. It hadn't been fair to Rachel nor Willow and I felt like an ass for even trying. The only way to salvage the night was to let Rachel go home and try and make peace with Willow.

"That's my new roommate and she looked a little upset. I should go and check on her," I said.

"Okay. I can wait," Rachel said and leaned back onto the couch. Her blouse was half undone and I could see her bra peeking out of the shirt. I knew she had made the move on purpose. To entice me, but all I cared about now was seeing Willow and making sure she was okay.

"I think it would be best if you go home," I said.

"Why?" she asked, I could see she was pissed.

"I don't know how long I'm going to be with Willow and the mood is kind of broken," I said.

"Whatever," Rachel said. She stood up adjusted her clothes and with as much annoyance as she could muster in her walk, she stormed out of the house.

I felt terrible, I did. I shouldn't have done that to her. But it would have been worse if I had slept with her when I was thinking about Willow. I didn't know how to tell Rachel that I just wasn't into her, that I was only thinking about and wanted to be with another woman. I was sure that Rachel would hate me, would never talk to me again, and might talk crap about me to my friends. It was all things that I deserved, but I could only hope she would find someone else soon and get over me. I had a feeling she would.

With one woman taken care of, or at least out of the house, it was time to deal with the more pressing issue. With the woman that had been occupying my mind and who I had hurt when she had walked into the house. I adjusted myself and took a few deep breaths before I walked up to her door and knocked on it.

"Willow?" I called out.

"I'm fine," she said, but the way she said it told me she wasn't.

"Can I come in?" I asked.

"No," she said, more like she almost bellowed it.

"Please. I'd like to explain," I said.

She didn't answer me and I started to worry that she wasn't when I heard her say softly, "Come on in."

I opened the door slowly and walked in. I had not been in the room since she took it over. I didn't feel it was right to be in her space and wanted to feel that she had some privacy. I hadn't expected her to do much to change the place, but she had. She had decorated the walls with pictures of different European cities, all in different seasons and times of the day. It gave a feeling like you were on vacation when you looked at the posters. She had changed the lampshade on the lamp on the bedside table giving a soft glow to the room. The bed was covered in a soft green and blue bedspread that helped to give the room a homey feel.

Willow was sitting up on the bed with her back pushed up against the wall, her legs were stretched out in front of her. She hadn't changed out of her work clothes, but she had taken off her shoes. She was holding a tissue in her hand and her eyes were puffy and I could tell that she had been crying.

"I didn't mean to ruin your night," she said.

"You didn't. Not in the least," I said and sat down on the edge of the bed. I wanted to reach out and touch her. To put my hand on her leg, to give her a reassuring squeeze. But I knew if I did that, I wouldn't be able to stop. That I would keep going until I was lying next to her and kissing her. Until I was using my body, my mouth, and my hands to make all her sadness go away.

"I didn't mean to upset you," I said.

"No. It wasn't you. It was an awful day at work," she said and sniffed.

I went over and got some more tissue from her and handed them to her. Being careful that I didn't touch her when I did. "What happened?" I asked.

"It was just long and boring and hard and I didn't talk to anyone. They seem so busy they hardly had time to show me what I was going to do."

"Did you tell your boss?" I asked.

"There was no time. I saw her at the beginning of the day and in the end, that was it. I'm not even sure if I was doing my job right or why I was even there."

"It was only the first day, hopefully, it will get better. If not, then quit."

"I can't just quit. I just started the job; I can't go looking for another one. I have to pay my rent. I don't think you would take it too kindly if I stopped paying my rent."

"True," I said and tried not to laugh. "But if you aren't happy, then you shouldn't stay there."

"It's been one day. As you said, maybe it will get better. I have to stick it out. I made a commitment."

"I admire that. But you shouldn't be sitting alone in your room crying. You should come out, let me make you dinner or something," I offered. I hated seeing her looking so sad and all I wanted to do was take it away. If I couldn't do that by taking her in my arms, then maybe I could do it with some comfort food, or simple being a charming roommate.

"Thank you, but I'm not hungry. I think I'm going to turn in"

"Oh, okay. If that's what you want," I said.

I didn't want to leave her, she looked so sad, so lonely, so dejected. I wanted to make it better, I wanted to help her out, but I could tell she didn't want it. I wasn't going to push. If she wanted anything from me, she knew where to find me. I could understand her wish to be alone, even if I didn't like it.

"Well, if you need anything. I'll be right outside," I said and slowly walked towards the door. I half hoped she would stop me before I got there.

"Thanks," she said and gave a sheepish smile.

I didn't look back at her until I got to her door. "Good night. Sweet dreams. I hope tomorrow is a better day for you," I said and closed the door.

I turned around and leaned my head up against the door. I had no idea what it would be like to have a roommate but I had never counted on it being this hard. I couldn't go on the way things were. Things needed to change or I was going to go insane. There was something there between the two of us, I knew she could feel it. It was so evident when we were in a room together. I wanted to believe her that she was upset only about the job but I could tell it was more. That she had been upset to see me with another woman. Her reaction wasn't from someone who only thought of me as her roommate. That was the reaction of someone who was attracted to me. Who didn't like the thought that I had been kissing someone else.

It was all feelings that I could understand. I wouldn't have liked to have seen her kissing another man, especially in my house. It only showed me that something was going on between the two of us, and we needed to find out what it was. Though I had no idea how to go about that, as she clearly was still in denial. Conflicted on what to do, I headed to my room to come up with a plan.

Chapter 9

Willow

I couldn't believe that I had acted so childishly, so stupid, in front of Jay the night before. I hadn't known what to do when I saw him and the woman on the couch and thought the best course of action was to run away. I hadn't counted on the tears coming. On being so upset over the fact that Jay was with some other girl. Some woman who was much pretty and sexier than I ever would be. Of course, he would have someone in his life. Of course, he would be bringing them home. It was his house and he was a young, vibrant bachelor.

It shouldn't have surprised me. It shouldn't have affected me as much as it did, but it had. To make matters worse, he had been so kind, so understanding when he came into my room. I knew he still had the woman waiting for him, but he took the time to check on me. To see if I needed anything. There was no way I was going to let him make me dinner, even if I really wanted him to. Even if I had longed to have just that when I walked in the door.

But the last thing I wanted was to have to sit and make small talk with Jay and his woman as he tried to take care of me. I hoped he bought that it was work that was making me cry and not him. There was something about how he looked at me that made me wonder if he had. Not that it mattered, he had been quick to leave as soon as I gave him the out, telling me that he was only being kind. That he didn't want me to be upset and possibly leave.

It had been sweet of him to suggest that I quit my job. I felt like if I had told him I was considering it, he would have supported me. That he might even have let me slide on the rent until I found the right job. But I didn't want to do that. I had chosen to come out and I took the job, I needed to stick with it. I couldn't be throwing in the towel after only one day. What I did need to do was realize that there was never going to be anything between Jay and me. If he had any interest in me, he never would have brought a woman home. The sooner I realized that the better off we both would be.

It took a long time for me to go to sleep but when I did, I slept like the dead. I woke up refreshed and ready to start the day. It took it as a small blessing when I got up, a bit earlier than I had the day before, to find that Jay was not in the kitchen. I didn't want to talk to him. I just wanted to get to work and hopefully have a better day. I grabbed a granola bar and a banana and went to catch the train.

My boss, Cathy, was in a better mood when I walked into the office and saw her. It might have helped that I was thirty minutes early. She went with me to get a cup of coffee in the break room and to ask me how my first day went. Instead of telling her about my frustrations and annoyances, I asked her questions about my work and what I could do to make it better. She seemed to appreciate it and was happy to help me. By the time the office had opened for the day, I felt like I had a better grasp of what was needed of me.

The day passed by quickly, and I even was able to have lunch in the break room and talked to a few of my co-workers. They all said they were swamped because there was a case that was coming up that everyone was worried about. They told me that the office was not generally like this and that it would calm down soon. It made me feel better about the job and my role in the company.

No matter how busy I was, my mind kept going back to seeing Jay in the living room. To the woman he was with, to how he had looked when he had been sitting on my bed. I had come to Los Angeles to start a new life, to have a career, or at least to try something new. I had never thought that would include a man. I hadn't even thought about it. With everything that was going on in my life, it was best that Jay and I hadn't started something. He had given me a chance by taking me in, by letting me stay at his place. He could have picked any number of people I'm sure, but he chose me. I needed to respect that. And that fact that he wasn't interested in me.

As I walked out of the office for the night, the last thing I wanted to do was have a repeat of the night before. I was working on getting over my infatuation with Jay, but I didn't think I could handle seeing him with another woman. I felt more energized at the end of the night than I had the previous one and decided to go and check out the local restaurant near our house. The fact that I was doing it specifically to avoid seeing Jay was not lost on me.

Jay had shown me around the area a bit and I had seen a few restaurants and bars that I wanted to check out. I went into a bar called McCarthy's. Jay had pointed it out saying it had a friendly atmosphere and played some up and coming bands on the weekends. It was a Tuesday and didn't expect to find a band, but that was fine. I was just looking for a place to have a drink.

I walked in McCarthy's and realized it was smaller than it looked from the outside. It had a dark brown wood bar the lined the right side of the bar, with barstool sitting in front of them. There were the typical neon signs along the walls and a few flat-screen televisions. Off to one side there was a small pool table with high top tables surrounding it. In the very back there was a small bandstand.

"What can I get for you?" the bartender said as I walked up to the bar.

"Um? A beer please," I said.

"Got a particular one in mind? Or do I get to pick for you?"

"Sorry. Yes. I'll have a Stella please," I said and shook my head as he went to get the drink.

"First time here?" he asked as he put the drink down in front of me.

"Yes. First time in a bar by myself," I admitted. I was surprised I had, but there was something about him, that made it easy to talk to him.

"Well, we are glad that you're here. Can I get you a menu?" he asked.

"Just the beer for right now," I said and saluted him with it before taking a drink.

"No problem, let me know if you need anything else," he said and walked away.

I leaned back into the chair and looked around me. The place was decently busy for Tuesday. There were a few tables that had other patrons sitting around it and a couple that was sitting at the far side of the bar. I started to feel a little self-conscious because I wasn't with anyone and went to text Madison. She said she might have reception when she was in some ports but I couldn't remember what days she was on land. It didn't surprise me that she didn't respond to my texts, even if she was on land, I was sure she was out doing something fun. And I tried to convince myself that I was too. I should be out., I should be making friends. I should be seeing the city that I was going to call my own. There was no time like the present so I called over the bartender and told him I wanted to see the menu. I had told myself I should try and find a local bar, one that I could go to and feel comfortable in. I couldn't do that if I only had one drink and left.

After two beers and a juicy burger later that I went home. I had ended up having a few brief conversations with Alex, the bartender, and felt comfortable enough that I might go back again. When I left the bar, it was late, and I hoped it was late enough that Jay would already be in bed. I knew I was going to run into him, that I was going to have to talk to him eventually. I wasn't ready for it yet. I had such a nice day, I wanted to keep it that way. I didn't want to change that by having an awkward conversation with Jay. I hoped to just sneak into the house, take a shower and call it a night.

Luck was not on my side for as I walked into the house, it was to see Jay sitting in the living room, reading a book.

"There you are," he said.

He said it in such a way that I wasn't sure if he had been worried about me or if he just realized that I wasn't home. Not that it mattered one way or the other.

"Yeah. I hope I'm not interrupting anything," I said and took off my coat.

"What? No. Definitely not," he said.

"Oh okay, " I said, for lack of anything better to say.

"How was your second day at work?" he asked. He turned around on the couch so he could see me easier.

"It was good. A lot better than yesterday. I talked to my boss and cleared a few things up and met a few co-workers."

"Was that who you were out with?" he asked.

I don't know why but I found myself saying, "Actually, I met a guy at work and he took me to dinner."

Jay couldn't hide the shock in his voice. "Really? Wow. Good for you," he said. Adding the last part slowly.

"Thanks. He seems really nice and I think we might be spending some time together after work, you know."

"Oh okay. That's wonderful for you. I should let you get settled in and I should be heading for bed myself. I'm glad you had a nice evening and things went so well for you."

"Thanks," I said. I was about to ask him how his day was but before I could, he got up and went to his room. I watched him go, a feeling of sadness overwhelming me. I couldn't understand why I told him I had met some guy. It was stupid. I didn't and I wasn't good at lying. But I hadn't wanted Jay to know that I had spent the evening alone, avoiding him. I didn't want him to pity me if he decided to bring anyone home, or for him to feel that he couldn't. If we were going to be roommates in the true sense of the word then we needed to get used to the idea that we were going to be dating other people. I might have pushed the hand a little bit on that one, but it seemed like the best way. Though as I went to my own room and got ready to take my shower, I couldn't get rid of the feeling that I had made a horrible mistake.

Chapter 10

Jay

I wasn't looking forward to going home. I wasn't looking forward to seeing my house empty again, to knowing that Willow wasn't going to be there when I got there. It had been two weeks since she had moved in and I had hardly seen her. Gone was the fun and enjoyable conversation we had on the first weekend. Gone was the ability to even talk to her in general about the day. Gone was the enjoyment I had found in knowing she was going to be there. I had initially been happy to have the place to myself, to not have anyone to worry about being in my space, using my stuff. But I liked having Willow around. I wanted more of that, had hoped I would, but it hadn't happened.

She was always with her boyfriend. Some man I didn't even know the name of, and I didn't want to. All I knew was that she was spending all her free time with him. That she was never home because she was with him. That for some reason she never brought him around to the house. I wasn't sure if she didn't want me to meet him, that she was afraid that I wouldn't like him, or that her new guy wouldn't like me. Whatever it was, the whole situation bugged me. There was something that was off about it and I couldn't put my finger on it. Or I was just upset that she was with someone and that someone wasn't me.

I couldn't believe that I had lost my chance to try something with her. That the minute I had decided to throw caution to the wind and see if we could be something, she up and got herself a boyfriend. One she wanted to spend every waking moment with. Willow was cordial, even friendly with me, but gone was the flirtation and teasing that had gone on between the two of us. We would talk as we were getting ready for work or if we passed each other in the hall, but that was about it. We hadn't shared a meal or gone to the Farmer's Market since the first weekend and I missed it, desperately. It was like she didn't have time for me and it sucked. I tried to tell myself it wasn't like we had something, we had only spent one weekend together, but it had been an epic weekend as far as I was concerned. I had hoped it would continue, but she hadn't.

The suggestions she had made for my screenplay went to good use and I was done with the first draft and was working on the rewrites. I had talked to my agent, who was excited about seeing it and wanted to start showing it to producers in the next couple of months. I was cautiously optimistic about it and knew that I had Willow to thank as much as anything else. But I couldn't tell her as she was never around for me to.

I had found myself needing to be out of the house, seeing friends, going to the movies, anything that I could so I wouldn't be in the house, alone, when Willow wasn't there. I spent more time with Charlie and had gone to a few parties at some friends' houses. There were a few women who had flirted with me, and I knew I could have easily gone home with a number of them, but I didn't want to. If I couldn't have Willow, I didn't want anyone. I hoped that eventually, that feeling would change, so I kept going out.

When Charlie canceled on going to the local bars with me, I decided to head out on my own. It had been a while since I had done it, and when I first moved into the house I had. I needed to get back into that routine, to being more myself. The screenplay and then Willow had sidetracked that a little bit and it was high time I changed that. I wandered down towards the restaurants and bars. I thought about stopping in at Rodriguez's, but I wasn't in the mood to listen to karaoke or Mexican food. Sully's was usually where Charlie and I would go to but that was because we usually played pool there. I wasn't feeling up for pool so I decided to check out another bar that I had never been to but had heard good things about.

McCarthy's was a bar that I had always thought catered to a rougher crowd than I was used to and liked to play music from bands I had never heard of. Recently, it had been bought out and I had been hearing that it was changing its look and style. I had told Willow about it when I gave her a tour of the area, telling her more about it than I actually knew. I had thought that perhaps we would go and check it out together one night, but then I had hoped for a lot of things that hadn't happen.

I figured, if I liked the place then I would bring Charlie back with me. McCarthy's was a bit dark when I walked in and it took me a minute to adjust my eyes. When they did, I could see the place was busy for a Thursday evening. There was a small stage set up in the back that had a few people working on it, making me think that there was going to be a band playing soon. The tables were pretty full that lined the walls and filled the middle of the room, but there were a few seats still available at the bar, so I walked up there.

"What can I get you, man?" the bartender asked.

"A glass of Downtown Ale," I asked, mentioning a local beer.

"Sure. Coming right up," he said.

While I waited, I looked around the bar. The place was busy but it didn't feel that way. I didn't feel crowded or that the people who were there were very loud. Instead, it had a cozy, comfortable feel to it. My eyes fell to a woman sitting by herself at the end of the bar. I smiled to myself and thought it was nice that the bar was a place that a woman could go, have a drink by herself, and not feel that she was going to be harassed. I never worried about coming into a bar alone, but it made me like the bar even more that women could do the same.

There was something about the woman that looked familiar and I felt ridiculous, but I wanted to go up to her and ask if I knew her from somewhere, but I wasn't going to do that. Besides the fact that I could be wrong, I didn't want the woman to think that I was hitting on her. But then she lifted up her head and my breath caught in my throat. It was Willow, I was sure of it. But it didn't make sense to me. She had said she was going to be hanging out with her boyfriend. She had made me think that they were going to stay close to their work. If that was the case, why was she here?

I thanked the bartender for the drink and asked him to open up a tab as I handed him my credit card. With a drink in hand, I walked over to the other side of the bar and Willow.

"Willow?" I asked as I approached her.

"Jay? What are you doing here?" she asked.

"I wanted to get a drink, so I thought I would try this place out. What are you doing here?"

"Dan wasn't feeling well, so I decided to have dinner here," she said.

"You should have told me, I would have joined you," I said and sat down next to her.

She eyed me as I did and I wondered if she didn't want me to sit with her. "Is it okay if I join you? Were you with someone else?" I asked.

"No. No, it's fine," she said.

"Have you come in here before?" I asked.

Before she could answer, the bartender came by with another drink for Willow. "Saw you were getting low," he said and placed a beer on the bar in front of her. "The burger should be coming right up," he added.

"Thanks, Alex," she said.

"I take it you have," I said.

"A few times," she replied.

I assumed she had come here with Dan, her boyfriend, but I didn't want to know. Instead, I asked, "Is the food good here?"

"Extremely," she said.

I reached over and glanced at the menu. When Alex came back with Willow's dinner, I asked for one of the same.

Willow bit into her burger and I reached over and took a fry. She looked at me sideways when I did and I stopped halfway through my bite. "Can I have one?" I asked.

She laughed as best she could through her burger. She finished her bite and said, "A little late for that don't you think?" she asked.

"I'll share mine with you when they come," I offered.

"Deal," she said.

The rest of the night passed in a blink of an eye. It was like how it had been the first weekend she had moved in. We talked easily to each other. She told me about how challenging her work was, but that she was enjoying it and that she found it rewarding. I told her how the screenplay was going and the changes she had suggested that I had put in. Occasionally, Alex would come over and talk to us and at one point asking Willow if I was bothering her.

"No. He's my roommate," she said.

"Oh. Hey. Nice to meet you, I'm Alex," Alex said.

"Jay," I said and extended my hand.

"Good to have you here," he said. There was something in how he said it that made me wonder how often Willow was at the bar by herself or if Alex just liked having locals hanging out at the bar. I didn't get a chance to question it further as Willow and I got back to discussing my screenplay.

It was late when we left the bar, telling Alex that I would be back soon. He hugged Willow when we left. The street was deserted as we walked back to our place. I walked on the outside of the sidewalk, keeping Willow close to me. I wanted to reach out and take her hand. I wanted to stop her in our walk and kiss her in the moonlight, but I couldn't do any of that. She had a boyfriend and was clearly not interested in me. We chatted easily as we had all night, but there was still something that didn't seem right in the back of my head and I couldn't for the life of me figure it out.

Chapter 11

Willow

I couldn't believe that Jay had found me at McCarthy's. When I saw him walking towards me, I thought for sure my ruse was up. I counted myself lucky that he believed me when I said that Dan had canceled on me. There were times when Jay had looked at me, and especially when Alex came up and talked to us, that I thought for sure he had figured it out.

For the last two weeks, I had been going to McCarthy's almost every night after work. At first, it was because I wanted to stay away from Jay. That I wanted to try and get my feelings under control. But the more time I spent at the bar, the more I liked being there. Alex was there most nights unless he had class. We had gotten to know each other, along with the owner of the bar and his girlfriend, Chloe. She was a physician's assistant at a local clinic and we actually had a lot in common as we complained about our jobs and our bosses.

Things were getting better between Jay and I. I had started spending more time with him, or at least not hiding from him if he was home. We had gotten on a slightly better footing than when I first moved in. He hadn't had any other women over and from what I could tell he had been home every night. It was odd to me, I thought for sure he would have had women lining up around the block to be with him. He hadn't asked much about Dan, my imaginary boyfriend, and for that I was glad. It was hard enough lying to him without having to come up with more lies.

I was getting to the point that I didn't like lying to Jay anymore. That it didn't feel right, and I was contemplating telling him that Dan and I had broken up. I felt like I could be around Jay without thinking about what it would be like to be his girlfriend, to be able to go to McCarthy's and hang out with him. Not wishing when we walked home at the end of the night that he would hold my hand.

All my good intentions and hard work left after spending one evening with Jay at McCarthy's. It was like I had always wanted and imagined it. We chatted, laughed, and teased each other. I had wanted to know how his screenplay was going, but I had been afraid to ask. At McCarthy's, he had talked about it for hours. I was surprised at how many of my suggestions he had used and that he was so hopeful that he was going to get someone interested in it. I had been happy for him and excited that my suggestions had helped him so much. He had been equally happy for me and how well things were going at work. It had been a wonderful evening, even walking home had been like a dream.

It would have been so easy to think that we were dating, that we were walking back to our place. That we going home to sleep in the same bed. But it wasn't true, and it was never going to be true. I had learned a lot from seeing and hanging out with Jay the night before. One I wasn't over him, not by a long shot and I needed to still take some time before I would even think about hanging out with him again. For now, Dan was going to have to stick around for a little while longer.

Jay didn't seem to feel the same way, for he had started texting me again throughout the day. I had responded when I could, trying to keep it friendly with him like we had the night before. When he had texted asking if I wanted to have dinner with him at the house, I had turned him down. Saying I had missed Dan and I wanted to spend some time with him. He had been so quick with the texts before that I could tell that he hadn't liked my response as I didn't hear from him after that. I couldn't figure out what problem he would have with me dating someone. It wasn't like we had ever talked about it, besides him saying he rarely had anyone over. He had had a woman over, I wasn't home a lot so he could be going on dates all the time. That was his choice, his right, as it was mine to make him think I was with someone too.

His reaction was still on my mind when I walked into McCarthy's after work. I smiled at Alex as I walked in and he looked around the person he was talking to as he waved back. As I walked towards him and the other patron a feeling of dread filled me. I knew who it was that Alex was talking to and it wasn't good. I quickly looked around, seeing if there was some way I could avoid talking to him, but before I could even simply turn around and walk out the door, Jay turned around and smiled at me.

"Fancy meeting you here," he said.

"Hello, Jay," I said, and looked anywhere but where he was.

"Really? That's all that you have to say?" he asked, and held out the chair next to him for me to sit.

I sat, reluctantly and looked over at Alex for some help. He lifted his hands in the air and shook his head at me. He wasn't going to be any help.

"Guess you figured out I don't really have a boyfriend?" I asked.

"You think?" Jay asked. I had never seen him angry before, but I could tell he was upset with me.

"Let me explain," I started.

"Please, I would love to hear it," he said.

I started to speak, but nothing came out. I had no idea what to tell him. I couldn't tell him the truth. He wouldn't believe me, or even worse, he would think I was a fool and would make me move out. I knew I had screwed up, but I had no idea how to get out of it.

"I didn't want you to worry about me," I said.

"Worry about you? You think that I wouldn't have worried about you because you had a boyfriend?" he asked.

"You have a life and you've been so nice when I moved in with spending time with me. I didn't want you to feel like you had to do that all the time," I said.

"Did you think that maybe I liked spending time with you? That I liked hanging out with you?'

"No," I said. The thought had never crossed my mind.

"Well, I did," he said and I could tell he was hurt.

We stopped talking while Alex put our drinks down. But he was quick to walk away, and I didn't blame him. I wanted to do the same thing.

"I'm sorry. I didn't mean to offend you," I said.

"You didn't offend me," he said with a sigh.

"I just thought it was easier if I wasn't around."

"Don't ever think that. I like having you around."

"I didn't want to walk in on you and another woman," I admitted and took a drink of my beer. That was indeed true. I wasn't sure if I would ever be ready to deal with that.

"You have no idea how sorry I am about that. I haven't had another woman over since that night and I don't plan on it."

"That isn't fair. It's your house too. You should be able to do whatever you want, and you shouldn't have to leave if you want to be with someone," I said.

"You aren't getting me. I'm not planning on having any woman around or going to any other woman's house," he said.

"Why?" I asked. The question was out before I could stop it. I wanted to know, but I also really didn't want to know.

Jay put his head in his hands and laughed. I looked at him and wondered if he had lost his mind.

"Are we both really this stupid?" he asked.

"What do you mean?" I asked.

"I like you Willow. A lot. I shouldn't, I know that. You were like my little sister for a while. But when I look at you and I'm around you, I don't think of you as my little sister at all."

"Jay?" I asked.

"That weekend when you first moved in, I was attracted to you. I was attracted to you from the moment I saw you. But I didn't want to scare you away, so I kept my distance. But I liked spending time with you, and I thought you felt the same way. I thought something might happen the night you made the stir fry, but then you pulled away from me."

"I didn't pull away from you!" I almost yelled. When Alex gave me a shocked look, I lowered my voice. "You pulled away from me."

"You were tipsy, you even said so. I wasn't going to take advantage of you," he said.

"Take advantage of me!" I said and then covered my mouth with my hands.

I looked around the bar to see a few more people had started to look at us.

"She was kidding!" Jay said to the crowd and then we both started laughing.

"I thought you weren't interested in me. And then you brought that woman home, I thought for sure you didn't."

Jay didn't say anything for a moment, and he wouldn't look at me. When he did, his eyes were full of regret. "I shouldn't have done that. But the only reason I had Rachel over to the house was because I was trying to get over you."

"What?" I asked. What he was saying made no sense.

"I thought you didn't find me attractive. That you only wanted to be roommates. So, I tried to get over you in the worst possible way," he said.

"That isn't any worse than me making up a fake boyfriend to stay away from you," I admitted.

"I knew something was off, but I couldn't figure it out. Imagine my surprise when I asked Alex how often you came in and if you had ever brought Dan and he told me you were there almost every night, and he had never even seen or heard of a Dan."

"It seemed like the only way," I said.

"The only way to what?" he asked.

"To put distance between us. To get over my attraction to you," I said.

Jay reached out and put his hand on top of mine. I had avoided touching him if all possible, and as our skin touched, I was reminded why. The heat, the electricity, was there as much as it had ever been. If not more. I looked at Jay with a shocked expression.

"It seems that both of us really messed this up," he said.

"We did?" I asked. I was still trying to process everything he was telling me.

"Yes, we did. But I for one am not going to let another minute go by without kissing you," he said.

"You aren't?" I asked.

"If that's okay?" he asked and leaned closer to me.

"Yes. Please!" I said.

Jay leaned in closer to me. His hand still on top of mine. I felt he was doing it as much to keep me in place, as if even wild horses could move me. My eyes locked on his and he gave me the smallest of smiles as he looked down at my lips. They opened involuntarily; my whole body wound tight as I waited to feel what it was like to have his lips on mine. When he was inches from kissing me, I closed my eyes. Only to have the fly open when I heard Alex yell. "Get a room!"

Jay stopped and dropped his head on top of my forehead. I laughed as much because I was embarrassed as anything else.

"Shall we get out of here?" he asked me.

"Sure," I said.

Chapter 12

Jay

I was holding Willow's hand. I was holding Willow's hand after almost kissing her. I was holding Willow's hand as we were walking back to our place, where I was finally going to be able to kiss her.

The whole thing with Dan just hadn't seemed right to me and I needed to get some answers. After finishing as much as I could with my script, I headed over to McCarthy's. I was hoping that Alex would give me some insight into what was going on. I had expected him to tell me that Dan was a jerk. Or at least I was hoping that. Or that Dan wasn't around much and Alex thought they were close to breaking up. I hadn't thought Alex was going to tell me that he had never seen Dan and that Willow hung out there almost every night.

It was then that everything made sense. There was no boyfriend. She had made the whole thing up. It took me a bit of time to understand why and the only reason I could come up with was that she was interested in me. As much as I was in her and we had both been fools for far too long.

I had hoped that she would come to the bar, especially after she said she had plans with her non-existent boyfriend. It only confirmed my new knowledge that she was trying to avoid me. That the chemistry, the attraction that I had felt last night, since the beginning, was not one-sided.

It was torture waiting for her to show up. I was half worried she wouldn't and also concerned about what I would say when I did see her. As soon as she saw me, she knew her jig was up. I almost felt sorry for her, but it actually only made me care about her more. I couldn't believe that she would go to such lengths to try and not be with me. To try and fight an attraction that was so plainly obvious.

And now I was going home with her. Having almost kissed her, a situation that I could almost have killed Alex for interrupting. But it was going to be so much better when I kiss her for the first time in our house. Where everything started.

"I never thought our house was this far away," she said as we walked across the street.

"Right? It's taking forever to get there," I said and squeezed her hand.

"Last one there's a rotten egg," she said and broke free from my hold to start running down the street.

I laughed and then took off after her. She beat me, but just barely to the house. By then I was mindless of anything but her, having watched her sexy little ass in front of me the whole way home.

"Caught ya," I said as I stumbled into the house right after her.

"Do you now?" she asked.

"I hope so," I said and reached for her. She practically fell into my arms. I smiled at her as my mouth found hers. My hands going to her hips and holding her next to me. Needing to feel her next to me. Reminding me that this was real. That she was there. That I was going to finally know what it was like to kiss Willow Murphy. Her eyes closed a split second before my lips touched hers. I saw her lips part slightly and then I closed my eyes. Wanting to feel, smell, and taste every part of the kiss. Her lips were soft and yielding under my pressure. Her hands went up and around my back, pulling me a bit closer to her. She sighed softly as my tongue darted inside her mouth.

I had thought to take things slow, but the moment my tongue touched hers, I was lost. I became a madman, I needed to touch her, every inch of her. I needed to see her body, her breasts, her legs, her spread out in front of me. I intensified the kiss, diving my tongue farther and faster inside her mouth. Willow responded in kind, clinging to my back harder, her tongue moving just as desperately, just as urgently, like mine. She tugged on my shirt, desperate to get it off. I reached for her dress and bunched it up around her waist. When I had a good hold of it, I tore it off of her and then let her do the same to my shirt. I stepped back and looked at her. Seeing her beautiful breasts all but spilling out of her bra. My hands reached up and cupped them. She brought her hands up to mine, squeezing them as they squeezed her breasts. She arched her back towards me and moaned.

It wasn't enough. I needed to see more. I had to see all of her. My mouth dove between her breasts as my hands went to her back and unclasped the bra. When it fell between us, my mouth sucked on first one nipple and then the other. Her hands went to my pants and she started taking them off. I let her, my mind and body only interested in touching her, sucking her, feeling her in my mouth. She tasted so good, I wanted more, I wanted it all. Her hands made quick work of my pants and pushed them down around my ankles. She moved closer to me as she did and her hands went inside my boxers and to my cock. She wasn't tentative about what she did. She found my erection and pulled on it, hard. The feeling was so overwhelming, I almost came right then and there. I knew that we weren't going to make it to the bedroom. That I was going to be lucky to make it to the couch.

I kicked off my shoes and then pushed off my pants, my hands went to Willow's panties and tugged them off. She took my cue and then tugged them the rest of the way off as I did the same with my boxers.

"Come here," I growled at her and she complied.

I lifted her up and she jumped onto me, wrapping her legs around my waist as I walked us to the couch. I could feel how wet she was as I rubbed up against her. I promised myself I would last longer; I would have more finesse with her next time. But for now, the only thing I wanted was to bury myself deep inside her and make us both come.

She kept her arms wrapped around me as I sat down on the couch. Her legs bent down next to us and she lifted herself up. My right hand went to the back of her neck and I pulled her to me to kiss her. She complied and my tongue was back in her mouth, hers dancing and teasing mine. My hands moved down her back and to her ass, massaging it and squeezing it as she started to gyrate on top of me. I wanted to slap her ass. I wanted to see if she might like a little pain with her pleasure, but that would have to wait for another time.

Her hands went from my shoulders, down to my chest where she squeezed my pecs before moving down between us and to my erection. I was completely hard and half worried my size would scare her, but she only moaned into my mouth and squeezed me harder. Sliding her hand slowly up and down on me in the most exquisite of fashions.

"Now. I have to have you now," I said to Willow as I broke the kiss. My mouth went to her neck. Sucking and licking it as I moved to her earlobe.

"Yes. Yes," she said and lifted herself up and over me.

Using her hand, she glided me to her opening. Pushing me in ever so slightly before, putting her hands on top of my shoulders. She was tight but wet and I could feel her stretching as I moved inside her. I knew I should take it slow, give her time to get used to me, but I couldn't. I felt like I had been waiting my entire life to fuck her and I wasn't going to wait a moment longer.

I moved inside her, pushing my way in as her body opened up slowly for me. She felt so good and I wasn't sure how long I was going to last. It took all my concentration to not blow my load in her. When I was all the way inside her, I heard Willow sigh and I could tell she felt the same way I did. A feeling of connection, of right, of perfection. I moved my head between her breasts and twisted my head from one side to the other so that I could worship them both properly. They had tormented me for weeks. Seeing her in her tops, looking at her breasts from far away and never thinking I was going to be able to touch them. To knowing what they felt like in my mouth. Now that I could, I wasn't going to let the opportunity slip by. And they felt and tasted even better than I had imagined.

Gripping her hips tightly, I started moving her up and down on top of me. Her breasts bouncing in my face as she did. She arched her back and started making soft sounds in the back of her throat that grew higher and more intense the more I pounded into her. Her body opened up to me, accepted all of me, and it was the most glorious feeling I had ever had in my entire life. I clutched her hips tighter as I moved her faster and faster over me. I could tell by the sounds coming out of her and how she gripped my hair so tightly, she was close to coming.

A split second after I felt her convulse around me, I cried out and slammed into her one more time. Spilling my seed deep inside her as the most amazing orgasm of my life ran through me. I clung to Willow, holding her close to me as we slowly came down. When she was spent, she dropped her head down on top of mine and then rolled off of me and onto the couch. I dropped down next to her. My body was more relaxed than it had ever been.

Willow kept her legs on top of mine, her hands over her head, her breathing coming in short and fast as she recovered. I tilted my head and looked over at her, thinking she was the most amazing woman I had ever seen.

"Well, that was pretty awesome," she said.

"Yes, yes it was," I said, breathlessly.

"We need to do that again sometime," she said.

"Give me a minute," I said and she laughed.

"I wasn't thinking right this second," she said.

"Maybe I was," I said and looked at her sideways.

"Really? Ready to go again so soon?" she asked.

"As I said, give me a minute," I replied and dropped my head back down.

Neither one of us spoke for a few minutes. My hand reached over and ran lazy circles along her thigh. Even just touching her like that got me going again, and I knew I wasn't going to need as much time as usual to recover.

"Water? Do you want some water?" she asked.

"Yes, please," I said. I knew I should be the gentleman and get it for her, but before I could, she got up and I let her.

She came back with two glasses of water and I sat up to take one out of her hands. The water was the perfect temperature and I drank greedily and Willow did the same. She giggled when a bit dropped down between her breasts. I watched transfixed as she reached down to wipe it off and then rubbed it between her breasts. The image made me rock hard instantly and I reached behind her to put my glass on the table. I brought my hands behind her legs and moved her towards me. She opened her legs up so that I was between them.

She eyed my cock and smiled at me. "I see someone has recovered," she said.

"Have you?" I asked.

I didn't wait for her to answer me, but did what I had wanted to do for such a very long time. I put my mouth between her legs and tasted her. She let the glass slip from her fingers, barely stopping it from falling to the floor. Her hand went up and to my hair, pulling me closer to her as I ate her out. She tasted as good as I would have imagined, but she responded better and faster than I could ever hope. She was instantly wet for me and her juices started flowing out of her. Her hips moved in time with my tongue as I lapped her up.

"Jay. Oh Jay," she said over and over again as she moved next to me.

She tasted so good that I knew if I didn't stop what I was doing I was going to come right then and there. I wanted to be inside her, I needed to be inside her again. To feel her surrounding me like she had only moments before.

"Stand up. Turn around and put one leg on the couch," I demanded of her.

She complied. She didn't protest, she didn't say anything, just did as I asked, and that was as sexy as anything else we had done. She put her back to me, her left leg on the couch and her ass up in the air. I walked up next to her, my erection touching her before I did and she shivered in anticipation. I had hoped, I had wished, that she would like sex as much as I did, but I was starting to see, that she was as into it as I was, if not more so. Which only got my mind going to all the different things we could to do together.

"Are you ready?" I asked her. My hands moved from her legs, to her stomach, and to her clit, giving it a little twist.

"Yes. Please," she said.

My cock slid between her legs, feeling her juices surrounding it. I moved back and forth behind her a few times as my thumb pushed down on her clit. She jerked her hips, telling me as much as anything else she was doing, how ready she was for me. I moved my hands to her breasts as I pushed myself inside her. She was just as tight, just as wet, and just as ready as before. It felt like heaven when I entered her.

She pushed her body closer to mine, needing to feel all of me inside her. My hands massaged her breasts, my thumb and index finger finding her nipples and giving them a slight squeeze. She cried out and then sighed, telling me what I hoped. She did like a little pain. I put that newfound knowledge in the back of my mind. Telling myself we would explore that, extensively, later.

I started moving in and out of her, slowly at first and then faster and faster. She grabbed onto the edge of the couch, using it for leverage as she moved with me. Gyrating her hips with mine. Allowing me to slap in and out of her. Going fully, deeply, into her before coming back out. Soon, she was moving so fast, I couldn't hold onto her breasts and ran my hands to her hips, changing the position that she moved over me. She cried out, loving the sensations it caused her. She dropped her head down and moaned each time I entered her. Crying out higher and louder with each stroke.

I moved closer to her, making her take me even deeper and she took it, all of it, and loved every minute of it. She was so tight and I could feel she was close to coming. Wanting to make it even better than the first time, I reached down her stomach to her clit and pressed on it as I moved even faster inside her. She cried out and pushed herself into me one more time before she came. Her body convulsing around me as waves of pleasure filled her.

At the feeling of her coming, I went over as well. Dropping my head down onto her back and cried out with my own pleasure. It was even more intense, more amazing and more earth shattering than the first time. When we were both spent, I pulled her down on the couch with me. My arms wrapped protectively around her, my cock still deep inside her, and my head resting on her back.

I was too overcome to speak. To do anything more than hold her. I had known it would be epic to have Willow in my arms, but this was even better than I could dream and I knew it was only the beginning.

Chapter 13

Willow

"I need to go to work," I said to Jay.

We were laying in his bed, him half on top of me, doing just about everything in his power to keep me in his bed. He was currently running his hands along my stomach getting closer and closer to my breasts. His lips were nibbling on my ear, sending shivers of excitement to run through my body. Last night had been one of the most amazing nights of my life and I really didn't want to get out of bed, but I had a job to do.

"You need to stay here. In bed with me. All day," he said and sucked on my earlobe.

I grasped onto his bicep and arched my hips up. Jay let out a throaty laugh in response.

"Say yes," he said.

"I think I already did, multiple times, last night," I said.

"That you did. And think of all the fun you could have by saying it again now, and later, all over the house," he said.

He sat up and loomed over me. His green eyes looking directly at me. It almost took my breath away. I wanted to stay. I wanted to feel his arms around me again. I wanted to kiss him, to hold him, to feel him so deep inside me I didn't know where he started and I ended.

"I want to stay, you know I do, but I have to get to work. And you have a screenplay to work on," I said.

He dropped his head down onto my shoulder and let out a soft sigh.

"You're right," he said and rolled off of me.

I felt the loss through my entire body, making me almost regret my decision. Before I could change my mind, I rolled out of bed. Jay watched me, his eyes roaming over my body as I walked towards the door, naked.

He whistled at me, making me blush.

"Stop that," I said.

"Not going to happen. You're a sexy woman and I want you to know that."

"Thank you," I said in the doorway. I had one last glimpse of him, lying on his side as he watched me walk out the door. His body on full display for me.

I knew I had the stupidest smile on my face when I got into work. That I practically whistled through the day. I got a few looks from my co-workers, but no one said anything, until lunch. I was sitting at my desk going over some briefs while I ate my sandwich, when Kayla, a fellow co-worker, came and sat down next to me. We had worked together on a few projects, and she had always been helpful and friendly. She was about the same age as me, with long blonde hair that she always had it in an elaborate updo that helped to show off her long neck and deep blue eyes.

"Okay spill it," she said.

"Spill what?" I asked. Though I was pretty sure I knew what she was asking.

"Why you're smiling like the cat that ate the canary?" she asked.

I could feel myself blushing as images of what happened between Jay and I last night flashed in my mind.

"Let's just say I had an exciting night last night," I said.

"Do tell," she said and leaned on my desk.

I didn't know her very well and I wasn't sure how much I wanted to tell her or not. "I don't really want to talk about it," I admitted.

"I can respect that," she said and leaned back. "But if you ever do want to talk about it, or you would like to introduce me to his brother or friend, or whatever, let me know," she said.

"Okay, I will. How long have you been working here?" I asked. I had seen Kayla around and we had talked about work stuff, but we had never had a personal conversation before and I was eager to make a friend in the company.

"It seems like forever but only about six months," she said.

"Really? You look so together, I would have thought it was longer," I said.

"Thanks. I'm good at faking it," she said and laughed.

We spend the rest of our lunch chatting, talking about where we had worked before, why we were there, and a little bit of gossip about our co-workers.

When Kayla got up to go back to her desk she said, "You shouldn't always eat at your desk. There are some great restaurants and shops around here. You should check them out."

"I'm not a big fan of eating alone," I admitted.

"Perfect. Me neither, so we can go together. Tomorrow?" she asked.

"Sure. I'd like that," I said and went back to work.

I had never been happier to have the day be done as I did that day. I could hardly wait for it to be five o'clock so that I could head back to Jay. We had been texting throughout the day. Letting each other know how our days were going. But it wasn't the same as being with him, talking to him face to face, being able to reach across whenever I wanted and kiss him. I had just closed my computer down when I got a call from Cathy, asking me to come into her office.

A feeling of dread filled me. I was worried that I had done something wrong. I had only worked for the company for a few weeks and while it was arduous work, I liked it. I was starting to feel comfortable and I had even made a friend. I was worried that I was going to be reprimanded for something or worse they were going to fire me. With a feeling of trepidation, I walked into Cathy's office.

"You wanted to see me?" I asked when I opened the door.

"Yes, please, have a seat," Cathy said.

"Did I do something wrong?" I asked.

"Goodness. No. Not at all. It's actually the exact opposite. I wanted to let you know that I have been watching you, as have some of the other lawyers and we're extremely impressed with how well you have done."

"Thank you," I said.

"Now, I'm not sure what your situation is at home, or how you would feel about relocating, but we have another branch in San Francisco that we going to be opened soon and we're looking to put some of our current staff up there. We think it would make the transition better and smoother and you were one of the people that we thought might be interested. It wouldn't be for a couple more months, and it would be the same position you have right now, but with a slight bump in pay. But it would have the potential to grow into something more."

"Wow. Really? Um, thank you," I said again for lack of being able to think of anything else to say.

"This is all in the early stages and we're still figuring out the logistics, but I wanted you to be aware and to think about it. As it gets closer to the opening, I will discuss your options with your further. We would, of course, pay for your move or any other expenses that you might occur. But that's something we can discuss later. I just wanted you to know and that we are delighted that you're here with us."

"Thank you. I really like working here, and I appreciate the opportunity." I said and shook her hand.

I was in a daze as I waited for the train, I couldn't believe how well the last twenty-four hours had gone. Not only was I sleeping with Jay and was almost guaranteed to do it again tonight, but I also made a friend at work, and there was the possibility of a promotion. I was ecstatic that Cathy felt so highly of me that they wanted me to help start up their new office, but I wasn't sure if I wanted to move. As much because I didn't want to think about leaving Jay. He was so wonderful and I loved spending time with him. I had no idea how long this was going to last, but it certainly wouldn't if I were to tell him that I might be moving in a few months. I wanted to talk to him about it, I wanted him to be as excited as I was, but I knew I couldn't tell him. I felt a bit like I was lying, but I rationalized that nothing was certain, not even he and I, and there was no point in stirring things up if I didn't need to.

The train seemed to take forever to take me home and I all but ran to the house. I threw open the door and called out to Jay. I looked around and didn't see him. I thought it was odd as he had told me he was going to be home all day and I thought for sure he would be there waiting for me.

"Out here!" he called from the backyard.

"There you are," I said to him as I walked out and then stopped in my tracks. He was sitting on the patio with a bottle of wine open and two glasses. Between them was a plate of fruit, cheeses, and meat.

"What is all this?" I asked.

"I thought it might be nice for us to sit out here tonight," he said.

"That's so sweet of you," I said and walked up to him.

He smiled at me as I put my hands around his face and dropped a kiss on his lips. His hands immediately went to my ass and gave it a good squeeze. I moaned into his mouth and opened my legs up so that I could straddle him. This was what I had been missing, this is what I had been craving all day. Even though I had only left his bed hours ago, I still craved him, needed him, wanted him, with a fever that was hard to contain.

The desire to have him, to have him take me right there in the backyard was so overwhelming. I rubbed my body up against Jay, feeling his erection grow as I did. His hands turned from soft and gentle to strong and possessive. I could feel his need for me. His hands moved to my hips, lifting my dress up and over my head, only breaking our passionate kiss long enough to take it off. My hips continued to move up and down on him as his hands found my bra and took it off. As soon as it was free, his mouth was on my right breast licking it and sucking on my nipple. I arched my back into him. My hands going to his head and pushing him closer to me.

"Yes, Jay. Oh, yes!" I cried.

"You feel so good. You taste so good," Jay moaned. His hands moved to my ass, giving it a tight squeeze as he lifted my hips up and down over him.

I was so wet and so turned on by him. I needed to have him then. I needed to feel him inside me. I needed to find the release that he was so good at giving me. I reached down to take off his pants, lifting my body away from him so that I could. Jay tugged on his pants just enough so that they were out of our way and his cock sprung out strong and proud between us. I reached for it and licked my lips as I gave it a slow, steady pull.

Jay tilted his head back and moaned. His hands going to my hips again and lifting me up and over him. He didn't have to tell me what he wanted, what he needed me to do. I already knew and was all for it. I moved my thong out of the way, telling him with my actions to take me and take me now.

He helped to move my body so that I was right over him, his cock inches from my center. I shuttered in excitement and anticipation of feeling him inside me. Of being one with him, of having him pleasure me so thoroughly. He used his hands on my hips to slowly glide me down on top of him. My body opened up for him effortlessly. It felt so good as if we had been made for each other. No man had ever felt so good, so right, so perfect as Jay did. Jay looked up and our eyes locked as he went deeper and deeper inside me. His hands slowly increasing the speed that he moved me in and out of me.

Soon, I was bouncing up and top of him, my body tightening around him as my orgasm grew and grew. I kept my hands on his shoulders, using them as leverage to help increase the tempo. I could feel my body starting to go over and I knew it was only a matter of seconds before I went over completely.

"Jay, yes, yes, yes!" I cried out as I came. My body folding onto itself as wave after wave of pleasure filled me. I had never come so hard or so fast before and the feeling was as shocking as it was exciting. Jay kept his hands on my hips as I went over, his eyes looking at me and giving me a wicked smile. It was only when I started to come down that I understood the smile.

He was still very deep and very hard inside me. I was shocked by his self-control, the restraint, that he was able to have. I certainly didn't have it with him. I became a wanton madwoman when I was in his arms. All I cared about was finding my release as quickly as possible. He did that to me and I couldn't be happier about it.

"Are you okay?" I asked.

"So good. And about to be better," he said.

I dropped my head down and kissed him. I loved having him still inside me, his arms holding me so possessively. There was something about it that was so freeing and erotic that it started to turn me on and I could feel myself responding to him all over again. Our tongues danced around each other, kissing deeply and passionately. My hips started to move over him again and I cried out when his hands massaged my breasts.

"Yes. Like that. I want to watch you come again. I want to hold you in my arms while I fuck you senseless," Jay said. His mouth went to my neck and sucked on it, biting the side before working his way down to my breasts. Taking one nipple in his mouth and tugging on it.

His words as much as his hands and mouth made me move faster and harder over him. He kept massaging and sucking on my breasts as I moved over him faster and faster. Where before he had set the tone, the pace, this time he let me. His hands were too busy on my breasts and then going down to my ass. His mouth sucking and teasing my breasts and nipples as I bounced over him. I closed my eyes as my body started to go over again. I had thought the first orgasm had been amazing, but I knew that it was nothing compared to what the next one was going to be. I could feel Jay getting bigger the more I moved and I knew he was close to coming as well.

"Yes. Just like that. Ride me. Come on, baby, ride me," he said.

"Jay. Oh, Jay!" I cried and went over the edge. Jay gripped onto my hips tightly, slammed me into him one more time and then cried out as he came as well. I wrapped my arms tightly around him. Needing to feel him as close to me as possible. He did the same, pushing his face between my breasts and turning to kiss each in turn.

It was a long time later that either one of us spoke, much less moved.

"That's one hell of a way to greet a woman when she comes home from work," I said.

"What can I say, I missed you. And I like it when you call this place home," he said.

"Well, it is," I said. I held back from saying that he was starting to feel like home for me, too.

"Good. I want you to feel comfortable here. I want you to be happy here," he said.

"I am. Extremely."

"Wonderful. Though I will say. I don't think I will look at this chair or this table in the same way again."

"Is that a bad thing?" I teased.

"No. Not in the least. Are you hungry?" he asked.

"Now, I am. And I should keep up my strength," I said.

"Yes. yes, you should," he replied and laughed.

"Come on. I'll make us some dinner, and we can drink some of the wine and the lovely plate you made," I said and got off of Jay.

He stayed where he was and I could tell he was admiring the view. I decided to tease him a bit and slowly walked over to get my dress. I bend down, making sure my ass was on full display for him when I did. He moaned and I could tell that he liked and was tormented by what I was doing.

"You keep that up and we'll never make dinner," he said.

"Just previews of coming attractions," I said and went to put on my dress.

"Can you leave it off?" he asked.

"Do you not like this one?" I asked.

"I like it just fine, but I would rather have you not wearing anything but your thong," he said and stood up and kissed me.

"It might make cooking a bit problematic," I countered.

"Don't worry. Any sauce or anything you get on yourself I will gladly lick off of you," he offered.

"Well, in that case," I said and walked into the kitchen, dropping the dress on the floor as I did.

Chapter 14

Jay

"Good morning, beautiful," I said to Willow as I wrapped my arms around her.

She snuggled closer to me, rubbing her butt up against me. I went from semi-erect to entirely in a blink of an eye. I growled into her ear and rolled her so she was lying on her back. Willow's laughter rang in my ear as I did. She was wonderfully naked and her breasts and the rest of her perfect body were on full display for me as I looked down at her. I loved how free she was with her body, with showing it to me. That she wasn't shy about being naked. I loved the feeling of her sleeping next to my skin to skin. My arms wrapped protectively around her as we slept.

It had only been a few nights since we started sleeping together and I was getting used to her being there. So much so that I wanted to try and broach the subject of her sleeping with me every night. She could keep her space and her stuff in her room if she wanted, but I wanted to be able to hold her like I did last night, to wake her up and make love to her, to be able to wake up and see her like this, every morning.

Willow's hands moved down between us and to my cock, giving it a slow pull. "It is a good morning," she said and smiled at me.

"Yes, yes, it is," I said and bent down to flick my tongue over her right nipple. It immediately became hard and she closed her eyes and squirmed underneath me. Her hands squeezing me even tighter.

My immediate thought was to grab her legs, lift them high in the air and plow myself into her. To bury myself in her so deep, to feel her surround me so tightly, so entirely, but I held off. There was time enough for that, but first I wanted to show her what I could do for her. What I could give her. I wanted her to know that I was the only man for her, the only one who could make her feel as good as I did. I wanted her to never be able to think or want another man besides me ever again. I had no idea where this intense possessiveness of her came from, but it was there. My need for her was constant. I had wanted her, craved her for so long and thought I would never have her. Now that I had her in my arms, I was never going to let her go.

I flicked her left nipple in the same way I had done the right. Marveling in her reaction. I could have spent all day, playing, sucking, teasing and licking her magnificent tits but there were other parts of her that I wanted to lick and play with too. I trailed light kisses and nibbled on her skin softly as I worked my way down to her center. Willow knew what I was doing and her hips started gyrating the closer I got. Her legs opened up for me, her body all but begging me to take her, to please her, to possess her.

Slowly, I worked my way to her stomach and her hips. Taking my time as my hands moved around her thighs and to her hips and then right near her center. I teased and coaxed her with my hands, my tongue, my mouth. Getting closer and closer to my ultimate goal. As I did, Willow cried out, squirming and moving her hips faster and faster. I could see, smell, and feel how aroused she was. I couldn't wait to taste her too. To feel her in my mouth, to watch her come apart right in front of me. I glided my hands under her ass, giving it a firm squeeze and tilting it up slightly. I could see her juices already starting to flow out of her, and I knew when I finally tasted her when I got my tongue on her clit, on her insides, and my mouth kissed her most intimate of places, she was going to come undone.

"Jay. Jay," Willow moaned over and over again.

I smiled to myself right before I flicked my tongue inside her. She was so sensitive, so ready for me that her hips shot straight out in front of her. I squeezed her ass again and brought her back down. She went willingly as if she knew that she was under my control, that whatever I wanted and asked of her, she would do.

"That's my girl," I said and had the satisfaction of feeling Willow relax into my arms.

Only to have her shoot right back up as I started licking, sucking, kissing and teasing her all over again. My hands massaged and kneaded her ass as I did. Feeling her come alive in my arms, in my mouth. She tasted so good, her reaction so amazing I could have stayed between her legs, loving her, all day long. Watching her, tasting her, feeling her only made me harder and I felt like my cock was going to explode it was so hard and in need of its own release. My hands moved closer to her back opening, wanting to tease her, to test her a bit and myself. I knew she had a kinky side, one that I wanted to explore more of. One that I knew would open up even more enjoyment for both of us.

Willow was twisting and turning beneath me, her eyes shut tightly and her body was wound so tight I knew she was close to coming. I lapped up all her juices one more time and then moved my mouth to her clit. My tongue flicked over it a few times and she cried out, moaning my name and twisting her head from side to side. My hands moved closer and closer to her back opening, as my mouth surrounded her clit and gave it a good suck. As she started to go over, I pushed one finger into her ass and watched in awe as she went over the edge. Her hips pushing into me as her body convulsed underneath me. Through it all, I stayed where I was. My mouth firmly on her clit and my finger in her ass. Slowly, as she started to come down, I teased her and me, a little bit. I moved my finger in and out of her as my mouth and tongue began to play with her clit again.

It got the desired reaction I wanted for very quickly, she was moaning underneath me. Her hips started to bounce under me and her juices started flowing again. As fun as it all had been, I knew I needed to take her, I needed to feel her surrounding me. I needed to bury myself so deep in her it was like we were one. Watching her come, watching her let herself go like that had been the most erotic thing I had ever seen in my entire life.

I moved my hands away from her ass and had the pleasure of hearing her protest. It only made me realize how much she liked what I had done and what I could do with that information at a later date. My hands slid up her legs, lifting them up and into the air. She was putty in my hands, her body sedate and willing in my arms. She smiled up at me as I moved between her legs.

"Jay," she sighed.

"Ready for some more?" I asked her and put my cock right between her legs.

She smiled at me and then closed her eyes, her head falling back. Telling me I was hers to do as I wanted. That she loved everything I did and was ready for more.

"I'm going to bend you in half and fuck you until you can't see straight," I said to her as I pushed my way inside her.

She was as wet, as tight, and as magnificent as I knew she would be. Her body opening up to accept me and tighten around me as if to tell me it never wanted to let me go. My body was on overdrive with its need to find its release. I didn't want to take it slow; I didn't want to take my time. I needed to be in her fully, completely and totally. There was no halfway now. There was only this, there was only her and I, and what we did to each other. What we would do for each other.

"Yes. Yes," Willow murmured over and over again and I moved deeper and deeper inside her. Her hips moved in time with mine. Her hands going to my back as she pulled me closer to her. Her legs high in the air, allowing me to go deeper and farther inside her than I had ever before. I knew I wasn't going to last very long, but I didn't want to go over alone. I needed to see Willow as she went over. I wanted her to look me in the eyes as she came so hard and so intensely that she would only want me in her bed.

"That's it. That's it. Come for me, baby. I want to watch you!" I cried out and plowed myself into her.

Willow bounced underneath me, our bodies in perfect sync. I could feel her body starting to tighten up and knew she was close, so very close. I bent down and took her left nipple in my mouth. Sucking on it as I moved over her. My body was so tight, just begging for its release, but I wouldn't let myself go, not until Willow did. When we went over, we would do it together.

My tongue licked her nipple before grabbing it between my teeth. As I bit down on it lightly, Willow cried out and came. Her body tightening around mine, sending me over the edge as well. My body slamming into hers one more time before I poured my seed into her. My back arched up, and I cried out her name. My mind going blank, my entire body consumed with her and what she was making me feel.

Totally spent, I collapsed on top of her and Willow dropped her legs down and kept her arms wrapped tightly around me.

It was much later that we got out of bed. It was only that we were both looking forward to going to the Farmer's Market again that we even considered leaving the bed at all. We had spent most of Saturday there, it was only the need for food and other necessities that we even left.

There was a hunger I had for Willow that was always there. I always thought I had a decent sex drive and that the women I was with still had a good time. But it was more, better, just greater when it was with Willow. I felt like she was awakening right in front of me. That she was allowing herself to be freer, to try things she never had done before, and it was a wonder to watch.

The sex was amazing, without a doubt the best I had ever had, but it was also the talking, the teasing, the snuggling, the waking up with her in my arms that as wonderful. I had enjoyed going to the Farmer's Market with her the first time, but I knew it was going to be even better this time. I could do all the things that I had longed to do. I could hold her hand, I could come up behind her and hug her, I could kiss her, I could tell people she was my girlfriend. All things that I planned on doing when we were at the market today.

"Do you want eggs or pancakes?" Willow asked as we walked into the kitchen.

"I can make the pancakes," I said.

"You sure? I don't mind doing it," she said.

"Why don't you make me some coffee," I countered.

"Okay," she said.

I went to the pantry and got out the ingredient for the pancakes. When I walked back out, it was to see Willow standing in front of the window her back to me, wearing only one of my T-shirts, as she poured water into the coffee maker. There was something about how she looked, how she was standing, the rays of sunshine that were shining all around her that just got to me.

As if in a trance, I walked up to her and put my arms around her. She squealed as I lifted her up and turned her around so that she was sitting on the counter.

"Jay, what do you want?" she asked.

"You. I must have you," I said.

"What about breakfast?" she asked giggling

"Later," I said.

"Well, alright then," she said and smiled down at me.

I couldn't believe I was so lucky as to have found a woman like Willow. Who was so willing, so free, so uninhibited. Who was willing to do whatever I asked, whenever I asked it.

The T-shirt had ridden up her as I had put her on the counter and I could see that she wasn't wearing any underwear. My eyes darted down to her naked bottom half and then back up at her. "Were you thinking this might happen?" I asked her.

"I hoped," she said and blushed.

"I like the way you think," I said and took off my boxer shorts.

She watched me and then licked her lips, the way she did, her eyes glued to my cock, which was fully erect between us. Watching her, watching me, turned me on even more. I thought to ask her to get down on her knees, to open up that sexy mouth of hers and suck on me, but I wanted to take her on that kitchen counter. I wanted to take her in every room of the house. To know that there wasn't a piece of furniture, that there wasn't a room, that we hadn't been together in. It was a goal I was more than willing to put my time and effort into accomplishing and knew that Willow would feel the same way.

"Come closer," I said to her and grabbed her ass so that she was almost falling off the counter.

She put her hands on top of my shoulders and looked down at me expectantly. I opened her legs up even wider for me. The countertop the perfect height for me to enter her. My cock quivered in excitement. My whole body on overdrive with need.

"Take off that shirt. Let me see those beautiful tits of yours," I growled at her.

She gave me a knowing smile then practically ripped the shirt off. My hands immediately went to her breasts. Touching them, kissing them, worshiping them. The way I went on, I would have thought it had been years since I had touched them, not less than an hour. But I wanted them and her so much, constantly, and I wondered if I would ever get enough.

Her legs went around my back, pushing me towards her as I kissed her breasts. I could smell how turned on she was and I knew that I was going to slip right into her body. That she would welcome me back and craved me as much as I craved her. I took my time entering her, wanting to draw out the pleasure, the excitement, the enjoyment, and the torture for both of us. I had taken her too quickly earlier and I didn't want to this time. I eased myself into her ever so slightly, only to pull myself right back out. Agonizingly slow, I moved my way deeper and deeper into her. With each thrust, each gyration Willow cried out, moaned and sighed. Her legs pushed me closer to her, her nails dragged down my shoulders and back. Showing me, telling me, that she wanted me, all of me, and she didn't want to wait. Still, I took my time. As much as I cost me. As much as I wanted to just slam myself into her, I didn't.

I was rewarded with the most amazing of pleasures when I was all the way inside her. There was something different, something deeper, more profound when I was finally completely inside her this time. "Oh, Willow," I sighed. Wanting to take a second to just enjoy this feeling.

But Willow had other ideas. She started moving up and down on me, frantically. My body instantly responded to her and I knew there was no holding back either of us now. My body moved with her, letting her take the lead as she bounced on top of me. She moved so that she was off the counter and completely on me. Her legs wrapped tightly around my waist using them as leverage to move her faster and higher on me. I wrapped my arms around her back, lifting her up and holding onto her ass as she worked her magic on me.

"Oh. Oh. Oh, yes!" she cried and slammed herself down on me one more time as she came. Her legs and arms wrapping around me like a vice.

At the feeling of her so deep around me, her body convulsing in its pleasure, I came as well. Crying out her name as I did.

Chapter 15

Willow

"We still on for dinner?" Jay texted asked me.

"Yes. I wouldn't miss it for anything," I replied.

I smiled at the phone and then put it aside. It was almost time for me to go home and it didn't surprise me that Jay was checking in on our night. Of course, I was going to be seeing him. There was no one else that I would rather spend my time with. It had been three months since we had started sleeping together. The weekend after we started, he had asked me to move into his bedroom with him, to sleep with him every night. I had happily agreed and had been sleeping next to him every night since.

My appetite for him in bed had only grown since we started sleeping together. He never seemed to run out of new ideas, of things for us to try and it had made for some exciting evenings and weekends. The three months had passed in a blink of an eye. We spend almost all of our time together, checking out local restaurants, sometimes doing cheesy touristy things in the area. We even went away for a weekend up to Santa Barbara which had been one of the best weekends of my life. I didn't know that I could be this happy that life could be this good.

Work was going well; Cathy had started to slowly give me more and more responsibilities and I felt more a part of the time team. I had gotten closer to Kayla and even had her over for dinner a few times with Jay. She still kept trying to see if I had a friend or brother of Jay's to set her up with. Jay had offered Charlie, but she had turned him down. Still, the four of us would go out on occasions and it was fun to see Charlie try and hit on Kayla, to no avail.

I had no idea that when I moved to Los Angeles that my life would turn out the way it did. I had never imagined that I would find someone as wonderful as Jay to spend my time with, who would get me, support me, laugh with me, talk with me and was there for me no matter what. I hoped I was there for him as much as he was for me. He had continued to work on tweaking his screenplay and a week ago had sent it out to his agent. He had been a bit stressed getting it finished and then waiting to see if anyone would be interested in it. I told him it was only a matter of time, but that was easier for me to say than him. I had offered to take him out to dinner tonight to get his mind off of everything.

If we weren't at home, usually in bed, or out exploring the city, we were at McCarthy's. I had hoped to find a place that I could call my own. A local pub to sit and have a drink at after work, and I had found that in spades at McCarthy's. I had gotten to know Alex better as well as the owner, Sawyer, and his girlfriend, Chloe. We even started to follow some of the bands that came in to play regularly and had become friends with them.

There was still the issue of the promotion or possible relocation at work. Just that morning Cathy had brought up the move to San Francisco telling me she would have a formal offer coming soon. I had smiled at her and thanked her. I didn't know what else to do. I knew it was an excellent opportunity for me. That I wanted to be a part of this company and wanted to see how far I could take it. But I wasn't sure if I wanted to move to San Francisco.

The biggest reason, the main reason was because of Jay. His life was in Los Angeles, he was on his way to becoming an important screenwriter and he would need to stay in the city to make that happen. I knew he would never agree to go with me, and I wasn't even going to put him in the situation to ask.

I had never thought I would put a boyfriend over my career and had always chastised women who did. But I had never thought I would have something as great as I had with Jay. Who I wanted and could imagine a life, a future with. I had fallen in love with him. I knew it wasn't logical, I knew it shouldn't have happened, but it did, and I couldn't be happier. We had only started dating, but with us living together it had felt like things had moved faster than usual. That the feelings had grown so quickly because we were always around each other. I wanted to continue to have him in my life for as long as possible.

It was too early to tell him, I knew that, but it didn't change the way I felt or that I was excited about seeing him and helping him to get his mind off his troubles.

"Big dinner tonight?" Kayla asked as we were heading down to the lobby.

"Yes. Jay has been so stressed about his screenplay. I thought it would be nice to get him away. Have a bit of fun. Get his mind off of things."

"You're such a good girlfriend. I hope he knows how lucky he is to have you."

"I'm the lucky one," I said.

"You two are so cute it's almost disgusting," Kayla said and stepped off the elevator. "Well, I'm off to hit a bar that's supposed to have the best happy hour. Which hopefully means it has the best men as well. I would have someone go with me, but she has other plans."

"I'm sorry. Maybe tomorrow?" I offered.

"You're forgiven. And I want to hear all about your special date tomorrow."

"Deal," I said and hugged her good-bye.

As I rode home on the train, I thought about what Kayla had said. Jay and I were a bit ridiculous in how happy we were, but I couldn't help it. I knew Kayla had some problems finding a man and that she was a little obsessed with it, and that was probably why she was always commenting on Jay and I. I hoped she didn't feel like I left her out of things or that Jay and I were throwing our happiness in her face. I vowed to try and spend more time with her and be a better friend. Just because I was in a wonderful relationship with a man I loved, didn't mean that I should neglect my friends.

I thought about different things that I could do with Kayla as I headed home. But, when I walked into the house, I completely forgot about Kayla. Jay was standing in the middle of the living room, wearing a suit, something I had never seen him in and surrounded by red roses. I had no idea how he was able to find so many roses or what the occasion called for, but I was beyond shocked. It was without a doubt the most romantic thing that any man had ever done for me.

"Jay!" I said and cover my mouth with my hands. "What is all of this?" I asked.

"Just a little token of my appreciation for you," he said.

"A little token!?"

"Yes. I wanted to fill the whole house with the roses, but the flower shop ran out. Next time."

"Next time? You mean you're going to do this again?"

"Yes. I hope I have many more chances to tell you and show you how important you are to me," he said.

"Jay. I feel the same way. You're the best thing that has ever happened to me."

"Good," he said.

I walked up and gave him a kiss, wrapping my arms around him and tried to show in the kiss how much his gesture meant to me. I could feel him falling into the embrace and my mind immediately thought about us making love right then and there, but Jay pulled away from me.

"As much as I want to continue that, we have dinner waiting," he said and motioned to the backyard.

I followed him outside to see that he had set up strings of lights all over the backyard, giving it a soft yellow glow. In the middle of the patio, he had draped a white table cloth over the table and there were two large candlesticks with lite candles in the center. I couldn't tell for sure but it looked like he had gotten Italian food from Carmine's

"Did you get dinner from Carmine's?" I asked as he pulled out my seat and I sat down.

"I know it's your favorite," he said.

"You really went all out? Didn't you?" I asked and lifted my glass so he could pour me some wine.

"It seemed fitting," he said.

"Fitting?" I asked as I twirled my pasta.

"We've been together for about three months now and I thought it was time that we celebrated us," he said.

"That's a wonderful idea. But I was supposed to be taking you out. I was supposed to be getting your mind off the screenplay. Not that I'm complaining."

"It's funny you should mention that," he said and took a slow sip of his wine.

"And why is that?" I asked.

"I got a call from my agent," he said.

"And?" I asked. I wanted to scream at him to tell me. I knew he had good news, but I could also tell that he wanted to draw it out, to keep me in suspense and to enjoy the moment. As annoying as it was, I couldn't fault him for wanting to have his moment to shine.

"There's a producer that's very interested in it. He's going to be sending it over to a well known director, that was all I was told, to look at."

"Jay! That's amazing!" I said.

I stood up and went over to his side of the table. He moved out so that I could sit in his lap. My arms went around him as I kissed him. He kissed me back with equal passion.

"It's all because of you. The script wouldn't have been half as good if you hadn't had given me your suggestions and insight," he said when we ended the kiss.

"No. It was all you. I'm just glad I could help you out. I'm so proud of you."

"I know I haven't been the easiest to be around lately and I'm sorry about that. But I want you to know how much I appreciate all you have done for me. Whatever happens next, I want you by my side for it. And hopefully, this is just the beginning. I don't want to jinx it, but I'm really excited and optimistic that this is going to be great!"

"It will, babe! I know it will. This is just the start. The sky is the limit for you!"

"I couldn't have done it without you. I wanted you to know how much the last few months have meant to me, how much you have meant to me," he said.

He hesitated, and I could tell that he wanted to say something more. I cupped his face in my hands and asked, "What is it? You can tell me anything."

"I love you," he said.

His eyes locked on mine and I could tell that he really meant it, that it was as shocking to him as it had been for me. That he was a bit scared about what I was going to say but he had to say it.

"Oh, babe. I love you too," I said.

"You do?" he asked as if he was astonished that I could.

"Of course! How could I not? You're the most amazing, wonderful, caring, sexy, thoughtful and all over wonderful man I have ever met."

"And you are the most beautiful, insightful, loving and amazing woman I have ever met. I love you so much"

"I love you so much," I replied.

I leaned down to kiss him, when our lips touched, his tongue plunged into mine. Where before he had been reserved in how he kissed me, he kept nothing back with this one. His hands gripped my hips and I could feel his erection started to push up in his pants. I rubbed my leg against him, wanting to stand up and straddle him so that he could take me right then and there. I stood up to do just that but Jay stood up with me. I started to protest but before I could, Jay lifted me up and wrapped my legs around him.

"Dinner is going to have to wait," he said and kissed me again.

With his arms holding me tightly to him and my legs wrapped around him, he carried me into our bedroom.

Chapter 16

Jay

I woke up with Willow sleeping soundly half on top of me. I lifted my hands up and ran them lightly down her back as I inhaled the scent of her hair. I couldn't stop the stupid grin that was on my face. Last night had been amazing, better than I had even hoped for. I had been thinking about doing something special for Willow for a few weeks. Not only because it had been so great having her living with me, sharing my bed but we were so in sync with each other and it was the beautiful combination of exciting and comfortable to be with her. I wanted to take a night, just the two of us, to show her she had come to mean so much to me in such a short period of time. How she had made my life so much better, better than I thought was possible.

She was so sexy, all I had to do was look at her and I wanted her. Sometimes as soon as she walked in the door. Being in our house all day without her, I missed her and I usually felt an overwhelming need to show her how much as soon as she got home. Luckily, she never minded and actually seemed to have as high of a sex drive as I did. But it wasn't just that. She was so smart and witty, I could sit and talk to her for hours, laugh with her as she would tell me stories about her co-workers or what she had seen on the train. It had been easy to incorporate her friends and mine into our mix. Making it even easier for me to see a future with her. I wasn't sure what that meant as of yet, but it was something that I wanted to explore.

I had been worried about telling her that I loved her. I had known I did for about a month. It kind of crept in on me to the point that one day I realized I did and then I couldn't remember a time when I didn't. But I was nervous to tell her. She had been a bit reluctant to even start anything with me because of our pasts, because of our parents. We hadn't let them know we were roommates, much less that we were together. It was something that neither one of us wanted to deal with. Our parents had not ended on the best of terms and there was still a bit of a feud between them. I didn't want that to cloud what Willow and I had, especially when we were just trying to figure out what that was.

Initially, I had planned the evening to be a way to say thank her, to tell her how much she meant in my life. I hadn't counted on it being a celebration about my screenplay until late that afternoon. When I found out, she was the first person I wanted to tell. In some ways, the only person I wanted to tell. That I couldn't wait to see her reaction when she found out. I knew she would be happy, but I hadn't counted on her being that happy. It was then that I knew I needed to tell her how I really felt. That I wanted to share every happy moment, every triumph with her.

I had been nervous right before I said it, but as soon as I looked into her eyes and saw that she felt the same way, all my worries fled. I should have known she felt the same way. It was evident in everything that she did for me, how she looked at me, talked to me, and supported me. I only hoped to have the chance to do the same things for her.

Willow stirred a little underneath me, rubbing her body up against me. I turned instantly hard, nothing new when it came to her. There was something about her that made me always want her, and it made me wonder if I always would. My hands moved lower down her body and to her ass, giving it a nice squeeze as I pushed her towards me. She giggled into my chest and lifted her head up.

Her smile was as wide as mine as she looked at me.

"Good morning," she said and moved a little so that she could slide her hand down my stomach and to my middle.

"Yes, I think it is going to be," I said.

I went to kiss her but was interrupted by a knocking on the door. I dropped my head down, trying to will them to go away. The last thing I wanted was to see anyone. I wanted to go back to what I had been doing and continue doing it all day. I hoped that it was Charlie and he would get the hint we were otherwise occupied and go away. I looked at the clock and realized it was too early for it to be him, and as the knocking continued and grew more insistent, I knew that whoever it was, wasn't going to go away.

"Who the hell can that be?" I asked.

"I don't know," Willow said and rolled off of me. "Whoever it is, is annoying."

"You won't get any argument from me on that. I'll see who it is and get rid of them. Don't go anywhere," I said and kissed her back.

"I'll be here," she said.

I quickly donned a pair of gym shorts and yelled at the door, "I'm coming." It didn't stop the person at the door from banging.

"What?" I asked as I opened the door. As I looked to see who it was, I knew I should have looked through the peephole and never opened the door. It was too late for that now, and while I recovered from the shock of seeing Willow's mother standing on my front porch, she barged into the house.

"Where is she?" Stephanie asked as she stormed around the living room.

"Who?" I asked. I knew perfectly well who she was looking for, but that didn't mean I was going to make it easy for her.

"Willow. Who else? That is unless you have some other woman in your bed? I wouldn't put it past you, you slut," Stephanie said and started marching down the hallway.

"Don't even think about going down there."

"I will go wherever I damn well please," she said.

"Not without my permission, you won't," I said.

She stopped in the middle of the living room. "Like you're going to stop me," she spat.

"What are you doing here?" I asked.

"I've come to get Willow out of this filthy place, and from under your clutches."

"My clutches? Really? You make me sound like some one-sided villain," I said.

"Where's my daughter?" she practically yelled at me.

"I'm right here," Willow said. She stood in the hallway, a robe wrapped haphazardly around her.

"Pack your things. You're leaving," Stephanie said.

Feeling the need to show a united front and not putting anything past Stephanie, I went to stand next to Willow.

"I'm not going anywhere," Willow countered.

Stephanie sighed and then looked at Willow as if she was a small child that didn't understand the ways of the world. "Yes, you are. I have no idea why you thought it would be a good idea to live with this rodent, but it can't continue," she said.

"I'm perfectly happy here and have been for some time. I'm not leaving," Willow said and reached down to take my hand.

My eyes darted to our entwined hands and up at Willow. I was shocked and ecstatic that Willow had taken such a dramatic stance with her mother. I wasn't sure if Willow was even going to tell her mother we were dating or how she would react to her mother being in our house. I hadn't expected her to be so blatant in her feelings for me. I squeezed Willow's hand and stared down her mother. Letting Willow know that I was beside her, no matter what.

"So, it is true, you fell for his charms. And here I thought you were smarter than that," Stephanie said.

"Stephanie, you're treading on thin ice," I said and glared at her.

"Oh, how cute. You're defending her. Like you actually care about her. Why don't you just say what this is really all about?"

"What the hell are you talking about, Mother?" Willow asked.

"You know the only reason he's with you is to get back at me. That he and his father have concocted some sort of scam to try and get back at me. That he's only with you because his father told him to. He thinks he can get me to stop fighting for the painting, well, he's wrong. They've both have been plotting for years to get back at me and they finally figured it out. And you fell for it. How stupid can you be?" Stephanie yelled at Willow.

The whole I idea was so preposterous that I just laughed. "You're delusional," I said to Stephanie.

"What's wrong with you, Mother?" Willow asked.

"He's playing you. Just like his asshole father played me. And I'm not going to let them get away with it this time. I'm not going to let them win," Stephanie said.

"There's nothing to win or lose. This is about Jay and me. We love each other and we want to be together," Willow said.

"That's right," I said, feeling the need to tell Willow that I was right with her.

"You don't love him. He certainly doesn't love you," Stephanie spat.

"We do. And nothing you say is going to change that," Willow said.

"Oh, so that's how it's going to be?" Stephanie asked and crossed her arms over her chest.

"Yes," I said and looked at Willow.

She looked back at me and nodded before looking back at her mother and said, "Yes."

"Well, then you leave me no choice."

I knew a threat when I heard one but I had no idea what Stephanie thought she could or would do to us.

"What do you mean?" Willow asked.

Stephanie gave her a smug looked, telling me that Stephanie was doing all of this as much because of the theatrics as anything else.

"I know that Jay has a screenplay he wants to be made. All it would take is a few carefully placed whispers and comments on social media and you would be blackballed in this town."

"You wouldn't do that," Willow said at the same time I said, "You can't do that."

"Oh really? Watch me. You have three days to move out or I will. The choice is yours," Stephanie said and without another word walked out the door.

Chapter 17

Willow

I couldn't sleep all weekend. I kept thinking about what my mother had said and being worried she was going to do make good on her threat. I couldn't believe that my mother had come into Jay and I's house, that she had said the things she did. I knew that she didn't like Mark, but I had no idea it was this bad. It was like she had a vendetta against him. That she couldn't see reason and didn't want to when it came to him. Their divorce had been contentious and it had dragged on for years. I was in college by then and didn't hear much of what was happening. As much because my mother had gotten so obsessed about Mark and the divorce that it was all that she could and would talk about. After a while, I just tuned her out. It was one of the many reasons we hardly talked after I left college.

It didn't make sense where she came up with this ridiculous notion about Jay and his father. I couldn't understand what would make her think such things about Jay. I remember her liking Jay, being kind to him when we were younger. It was ludicrous to think that Jay would have offered to have me live with him just to get back at my mother. He wasn't like that, and he wouldn't do that to me. All I could think was that my mother was insane or she was just in that much pain after the divorce that she couldn't see straight.

This might not have been how Jay and I thought our relationship would become but it was what we had. I loved Jay, I wanted to be with him and I wanted to protect him. I just had no idea how I could do both. I didn't doubt that my mother would do what she said. She was a woman with conviction, who never said anything lightly. I only hoped that maybe I could convince her that she was wrong about Jay. That he wasn't in some conspiracy with his father.

Jay and I talked about it all weekend. Barely being able to do anything else. He called his father to tell him what was going on, to get his side of the story. Mark told Jay that my mother was still trying to get a painting he had bought while they were married. It was the one thing they couldn't agree on and my mother wouldn't let it go. Mark said he offered to buy her out of it, but she wouldn't. He refused to let it go and neither did she. Mark was amazed to see that my mother would go to such lengths to try and get the painting. He said he would try and talk to my mother but didn't think it would help.

On the upside, he was excited to hear that Jay and I were so happy together and that he would do whatever he could to help us out. All except give my mother the painting.

"It isn't like your mother can really do that much damage to me. She's only one person," Jay said.

"If only that were true," I said.

It was Sunday afternoon, we had gone to the Farmer's Market, but we hadn't been as into as we usually were. We got the food that we needed for the week, but neither one of us had any desire to stay and listen to the music or go have lunch anywhere. We had gone home, laid on the couch and binged watched a few shows. We held each other, I could tell that Jay needed to feel as close to me as I did him. To know that we were in this together and that we would have to come up with a solution. We had made love with our usual fierceness, but there was a lingering desperation from both of us. Like we were both worried that it was going to end. That it could all end.

"What do you mean?" Jay asked.

We were sitting outside in the backyard, a bottle of wine between us. Neither one of us was hungry but we were in the mood to drink. The afternoon was warm and comfortable, making it easy to sit outside and enjoy the weather. It almost made me forget the problems we were having.

"She's spent the last two years building up her social media platform. She's considered a minor social media celebrity and has a lot of followers. Do you remember that company 'Rocks On?'"

"Sort of. Weren't they a mixed cocktail company? They had a monthly subscription for different cocktails. They would send you the ingredients you just had to supply the alcohol?"

"Yes, that was them. And you remember how they went out of business?" I asked and took a sip of my wine.

"Vaguely. Something about bad business practices?" he asked.

"Well, that was what my mother, all her followers, and her other social media friends wanted you to think. From what I could remember, a customer service representative was rude to one of her followers. Mom freaked out and started a campaign to end them. She got enough people involved that they had to shut down."

"If the company had poor customer service than maybe they shouldn't have been in business," Jay said and poured us both some more wine.

"That was the thing, it later came out that the woman who initially bitched about the whole thing was in the wrong and was rude to the customer service rep, not the other way around."

"Why didn't they say something, fight back?" he asked.

"Who knows. They probably thought like you did, that she didn't have the influence, that it would blow over. But it didn't. If that's what she can do to a company, imagine what she could do to your reputation. She could make it so that you are a pariah in this town. That no one would want to work with you."

"We can't let her win. This isn't right. I don't want to give up you, but I don't want to give into her demands either," he said.

"I can try and talk to her," I said.

"Do you think it will work?" he asked.

"I can hope. But to be honest, I don't think so. She already teased it in a post this afternoon," I said and showed him the post.

"Wow, that's a bit cryptic and I'm sure there are people who are interested," he said after he had read it.

"It already has 10,000 likes, so yes, I would say she has people interested."

"Shit," he said and stared at the number of likes.

"That's it. I'm going to call her," I said. I reached for my wine glass and downed the rest of it. Needing a bit of liquid courage.

"Should you wait a little while? Let her calm down a bit?" he asked.

"I can't just sit here and wait to see what she is or isn't going to do. I need to talk to her, straighten this out," I said and reached for my phone.

Jay reached up to take my hand and I took it readily. I squeezed it tightly as I waited for my mother to answer the phone.

"You better be calling to tell me you've moved out," my mother said.

"Mother, we need to talk about this," I said.

"There's nothing to talk about. How could you be so stupid? How could you be so naïve? Can't you see what they're doing? How they're using you?"

"You have the situation wrong, Mother. Jay hardly speaks to his father. And he would never do what you're saying. We didn't mean to fall in love. We certainly didn't do it to hurt you. It just happened. Why can't you be happy for us?"

"Because Jay doesn't love you. He's the spawn of that horrible man who I won't dignify by saying his name. He's incapable of love, just like his father. He can't love you because he doesn't know how. He only knows how to hate and he hates you as much as he hates me."

I moved away from Jay and started pacing. My mother sounded as delusional now as she did when she was over at the house earlier in the day.

"This is crazy, Mother. You're acting crazy," I said.

"Don't you dare call me crazy. I'm doing this for me, I mean for you."

"No, you were right the first time. You're doing this for you. For some strange need to get back at Mark and how he treated you. You've been divorced for years. It's time to let him and the painting go."

"I will never let it go. He ruined me. He ruined my life and now he's trying to get back at me through you. I won't let him do it. You need to tell me now that you're moving out or I swear I'll do it. I'll ruin Jay's life and make sure his father knows it was me."

"That's what this is really all about, isn't it? Getting revenge on Mark, and you think you have the perfect opportunity to do it with Jay and I."

"I'll use whatever I have to, I want the man to pay. I want him to suffer the way I did," she spat.

"But Jay is an innocent bystander in this, you have to see that."

"He's his son, of course, he isn't innocent. The apple never falls far from the tree," she said.

Her comment made me wonder what that said about me but I let it pass. One crisis at a time.

"You aren't going to let this go. No matter what I say are you?" I asked.

"No. The only guarantee that Jay has that I won't ruin his career is if you tell me right now you're going to move out. Tonight."

"It's too late to find a place tonight, Mother. But fine. You win. I've been offered a job in San Francisco by my company. I will take it. I will be out of not only Jay's life but Los Angeles all together," I said and waved at Jay as he stood up and looked ready to grab the phone out of my hands.

"How do I know that you mean it? How do I know you aren't just paying me lip service?" "You can come by tomorrow and you can see that I've moved out, see the offer letter," I stated.

"Fine. I'll be there in the morning. Jay and that letter had better be there and you had better not be," she said.

"I won't, Mother. You won," I said.

"Good," she said and hung up.

"What the hell are you doing?" Jay yelled at me as soon as I ended the call.

"I have a plan," I said.

Chapter 18

Jay

I paced my house waiting for Stephanie to show up. Willow had left that morning and I wasn't sure when I was going to see her again. We had talked late into the night, trying to decide what to do. I still didn't like Willow's idea of giving into Stephanie or at least making her think that we were. But I had to agree with her, to a point, that there was no reasoning with Stephanie and this would at least buy us some time.

Willow had been scared that her mother was going to do as she promised right then and there in the phone call. That she seemed determined to ruin my father and me, no matter what Willow did. She felt it was the only way to get her mother off our backs, at least for a few days. I didn't like giving into Stephanie, I didn't like her thinking that she had won, that for even a second we were going to give into her blackmail, and that was what it was, blackmail. But Willow didn't agree. We had argued about it into the night. About what to do with her mother, and the job promotion she told me nothing about.

"I don't even know if I was going to take it," she said.

"You still should have told me," I countered.

"Probably. But I didn't want to worry you if I didn't take it. It happened right after we got together," she said as if that was supposed to make everything better.

"Okay, I can see that, but we've been together for a few months now. When were you going to tell me about it?" I asked.

"I wasn't," she said and then lifted up her hand to stop me from talking. "Only because I didn't want to take it."

"Why not? It sounds like a great opportunity," I said.

"It is, but I didn't want to leave you," she said.

"Leave me?" I asked, thoroughly confused.

"Yeah. The job is in San Francisco, I would have to leave you," she said.

"What makes you think that I wouldn't go with you?"

"You would do that?" she asked. Tears glistened in her eyes.

"I love you, of course, I would go with you. You would consider not taking a job for me, how could I not support and move with you so that you could take a job?"

"I never thought of it that way?"

"Would you want to take the job? Is it something you would like to do?"

"It's a great opportunity and a chance to grow with a company that I've come to be very fond of," she said.

"Then you should take the job," I said.

"But what about you? About us? Your career?"

"I'm a screenwriter. Yes, it would be better if I was here, but I don't need to be. I can commute. I can video chat, do teleconferencing, or if need be, it's a short flight down to LA. I could go down for the day if I really needed to be there for a meeting."

"Really? You would consider doing that for me?" she asked.

"Yes. Absolutely. I love San Francisco. It might be fun to live there. Explore a new city, have a new adventure. It would all be worth it, if you are there by my side."

"Oh, wow. Okay. That would be great. I mean, that doesn't solve the problem with my mother, but maybe if she didn't know you were moving up with me. It could work."

"Can you see never talking to your mother again? Never seeing her? Of her never finding out about your life from any of your friends or family?" I asked.

"After what my mother has tried to do to you," she started.

"To us," I interrupted her.

"To us," she repeated. "I never want to see or talk to her again. But there's no way she wouldn't want to know about my life. She would find a way to see what I was doing. And it would only be a matter of time before she realized we were together and we would be in the same boat we are now. We need to find a way to get her out of our lives, forever."

"Yeah, I have no idea how to do that either," I said and pulled her to me. We had held each other all night. I didn't sleep much and neither did Willow. She was up early, packing up most of her things, or at least trying to make it look like she was.

"I'm going to need to stay away for a while. I wouldn't put it past her to have some of her followers or someone watching the house to see if I come back," she said.

"I don't like this," I said to her and pulled her into my arms.

"I don't either, but this is how it has to be, for now. We'll be in touch, and this is only temporary," she said.

"It better be," I said, but we still didn't have an answer to how to deal with her mother.

"Call me after she's gone and let me know how it went," she said

"You have those meetings all day today," I countered.

"Still, leave a message if nothing else. I'll sneak out and go to the bathroom so I can listen to it. If you don't, I'm just going to fret," she said.

"Fine. I will. I don't think it'll be anything more than her coming in, seeing you aren't here. Looking at the offer letter and then leaving."

"Let's hope that's all she does. Still, call me," she said.

"I will," I said and she started to move away from me.

"What? I got to go. I'm going to be late for work," she said.

"Remember, I love you. We will get through this."

"I love you too," she said and left.

Watching her walk out the door felt like I was watching a part of me leave. She had only been back in my life for a little while, but she had come to mean the whole world to me. I hated thinking that her mother could hate my father so much that she would want to keep us apart. I never thought that I would find someone as amazing as Willow or that she would love me back. As I waited for Stephanie to show up, I kept trying to think of a way out of this, besides just blowing up my career and letting her win, and vowing that I would do whatever I could to protect Willow.

"Nice. Boxes, that's a good touch," Stephanie said when she walked into my living room.

"She's packing. She wanted you to know," I said.

"It's a start, but she should be out of here. Completely," Stephanie said.

"You gave her the ultimatum less than twenty-four hours ago. She had to go to work today, give her some time," I said.

"Whatever," Stephanie said, showing me that I had at least won one round with her. "Where is this offer letter?"

"The copy is right here, with her signature. She's giving the original to her boss today," I said

Stephanie looked at the letter, reading it slowly. When she put it down, she said, "She'll forget about you in no time. You aren't good enough for her and she deserves better."

"Willow might. She's the most amazing woman I've ever met. But for some reason, she loves me and is willing to do what you asked to protect me."

"Can't protect yourself," Stephanie said with a shrug. "Just like your father."

"Dad's a decent man, who didn't deserve to have his ass handed to him the way you did in the divorce," I said. I didn't know a lot about the divorce except that it had been so bad that my dad had vowed never to get married.

"His ass? He took me for everything I was worth. I had nothing when he was done with me. Not even my dignity. And now he wants to take my daughter? That isn't going to happen. I won't let her be hurt the way I was. Not by anyone."

There was something in the way that she talked about my father. There was such hate but I could see under the surface there was sadness.

"You aren't over my father, are you?"

"Your father can go to hell," she said.

"That didn't answer my question," I said.

"Tell Willow she had better be completely out of here in a week or there will be hell to pay," Stephanie said and stormed out of the house.

"Well, that was an interesting change of events," I said to myself and sat down on the couch.

I was still sitting there when Charlie came in through the back door.

"Is she gone?" he asked, his head just peaking in through the door.

"The wicked witch? Yes, she left. How did you know she was here?" I asked.

"I felt her bad vibes all the way over at my house, man. That woman is bad news," he said and went and sat on the couch next to me.

"You don't need to tell me that," I said.

"What did she want?" he asked.

I told him and he quietly listened. When I was done, he let out a long slow sigh, "Dang. What do you think caused her to be like that?"

"You know, I was contemplating that same thing when you came in. I think she's still in love with my father," I said.

"Dude! How crazy would that be? That she was doing all this just to try and get his attention. It would make sense, man."

"Yeah, but how do I use that to my advantage," I asked.

"That I don't know, man. I mean you got this woman that you love, that you want to be with, but you can't. It's like star crossed lovers from the olden times."

Charlie always had some interesting theories, but this was a new one. "What do you mean?" I asked.

"Well, usually when things weren't going well for a couple they would just go off and get married. Elope. Then everyone was happy. Or at least that was how I think it was," he said.

"It doesn't work that way now," I said and then stopped. I jumped up on the couch, startling Charlie. "You know what! You might be on to something!" I said.

Chapter 19

Willow

"Kayla, thank you so much for letting me stay with you," I said.

It was after work on Monday and I was sitting with Kayla in her living room. I had told Kayla everything that was going on Sunday night and she had immediately said to me that I could stay with her until the whole thing blew over.

"It's my pleasure. I'm happy to have you here," she said as she sat down next to me and handed me a glass of wine.

"I have no idea how long I'll be here, but it shouldn't be long," I said.

"Stay as long as you need. And you may be moving to San Francisco soon anyways," she said with a pout.

"I know. It doesn't feel real that I'm going to be moving. I just got used to this place and all of you," I said.

"A lot of the staff that's going up you already know and I would have gone too if not for my mother," Kayla said. Her mother lived nearby in an assisted living community.

"I understand and I'm going to miss you so much. But you will have to come up and visit."

"Visit you and Jay," she said with a smile.

"Yeah, we'll see," I said.

It still hadn't sunk in that Jay had not only agreed to move up to San Francisco with me but that he wanted to and insisted that I take the job. It only showed me what a great man he was and that he truly did love me and wanted what was best for me. I still didn't know how it was going to work out. How he was going to be able to come up with me, not only with his work but with the whole situation with my mother.

Jay had texted me after my mother had stopped by, stating she seemed to be placated and that he would see me tonight. I had told him not to come but he wouldn't listen. I missed him and wanted to see him, but I wasn't sure how wise it was.

"Did you narrow down the places that you might want to move into?" Kayla asked.

After I had given my signed offer letter to Cathy, she had told me to start looking at some of the company subsidized apartments they had in the area. When I had told Kayla, we had spent the better part of the afternoon looking at them. They were all quite lovely, but I couldn't decide if I needed a simple studio or one-bedroom if it was for myself, or if I wanted a two-bedroom, which would work better if Jay came up with me.

I felt like my life was in limbo, that I couldn't really make any decisions. I had decided to go to San Francisco, but I still wasn't sure if that was the right decision. Was I just running away from my mother and the problems she caused? Would it be a good and fresh start for Jay and I? Would he even be able to come up with me? I didn't want to think that his reputation, his career, and everything that he worked for could be destroyed simply because he loved me. I wanted to be with him, but not if it meant him losing all of that. I liked his optimism, admired it even, but I couldn't see a way out of this. I figured if nothing else, I could move to San Francisco so I wouldn't be reminded of Jay and I if things didn't work out.

"Not yet. I just can't decide yet. I'm not sure if Jay will really be able to come up with me or not," I admitted.

"I know a guy who could help you wipe out all your internet profiles. You could go dark," Kayla offered.

"I'm not going to run away or hide from her. From this. The only way to really be able to be with Jay is to be with him, out in the open. I can't live like that; I won't ask him to live like that and we shouldn't have to."

"Fair enough," Kayla said. "So, what are you going to do?"

"I'm going to keep trying to convince my mother to stop this. Hopefully, make her see that Jay isn't like his father, or isn't going to do what his father did to her."

"And if that doesn't work?" Kayla asked.

"I have no idea. Maybe we can brainstorm some ideas when Jay gets here," I said.

"Have more wine, that should help," Kayla said and poured me more wine.

We sat in companionable silence as we drank our wine. I was lost in my thoughts of Jay, my move, my mother, and so many other things that none of them stuck around for very long. It was almost too much to think about, too much to worry about that my brain started to shut down. Kayla seemed to understand my need for quiet, to just be and think for a moment for she let me. Silently enjoying her own wine and flipping through her phone.

"What the hell?" she asked and sat up off the couch.

"What?" I asked.

"Um? I don't know," she said.

"Okay," I said and closed my eyes and leaned back into the couch.

"Oh, this shit just got real!" she yelled.

I opened my eyes and looked at her. "What's going on? What has you so freaked out?"

'I'm not the only one," she said and started to hand me her phone.

"What are you trying to show me?" I asked, and then turned when there was a knock on the door. "Hold that thought. That must be Jay."

"Good. Maybe he can explain what's going on," Kayla said.

I sent her a questioning look as I went to get the door.

"Hey, you," I said as I opened the door for Jay.

"Hey, back. I miss you," he said and drew me into his arms.

I hugged him back. Loving the feel of his strong arms around me, of the feeling of him holding me close like he never wanted to let me go. I clung to him. Realizing that I missed him as much as he did me. That he was so important to me that I couldn't imagine my life without him and that I didn't want to.

"Come on in. Kayla opened a bottle of wine," I said and lead him into her living room

"Hey Kayla," he said.

"Hey yourself," she said. She gave her a look like he had done something.

"Is it already out?" he asked.

"If it is what I think you're talking about then, yes," she said.

"Wow, that was fast. I thought I would have had time to tell Willow what I was doing," he said.

"What did you do?" I asked and looked at first Jay then Kayla then back again.

"I'm going to leave you two alone," Kayla said. She refilled her wine glass with a hefty portion of wine and then went into her room.

"Should I be worried?" I asked him after she was gone.

"I hope not. I hope that this will have solved our problem," he said.

"You figured something out?" I asked, excitedly.

"Don't be mad. And believe me, this wasn't how I pictured doing this. Or how I wanted it to happen, but I'll make it up to you, I promise," he said.

"What did you do?" I asked. Between his and Kayla's cryptic comments I was starting to get a little worried.

"So, after your mother left our place, I got to thinking and Charlie came over and we tried to come up with some ideas on what to do. I couldn't think of anything but then Charlie said something that just clicked."

"What did he say?" I asked.

"That if we got married, it would solve everything," Jay said.

"What?!" I yelled at him. Of all the things I would have thought Jay would say, that was the furthest from my mind. "What are you talking about?"

Jay reached up and took my hands in his. "This isn't how I wanted this at all. I imagined when I proposed to you, that well, I would ask you first then tell the world. That I would do it in the most romantic of ways. Telling you how much I love you. How much you have changed my life for the better. That every day is a blessing because I get to spend it with you. That you have made me the happiest man I ever could be and that I want to spend the rest of my life with you, making you as happy as you have made me," he said.

"Jay!" I said and could feel tears forming in my eyes.

"I don't want anything to ever come between us. Lest of all your mother. She doesn't get to decide our happiness or how we show our love for each other. That is for us. And I got thinking, what if we told the world that not only had we gotten engaged, but that your mother and my father were ecstatic about it," he said.

"But they won't be. Mother will freak out if she even thinks that has happened."

"She can't if we already told the world she was happy about it," he said.

"What do you mean?" I asked.

"I let it leak that we were engaged. Not only that, but our parents were excited about it. Look," he said and showed me the post.

Sure enough, there was what looked like an engagement announcement for Jay and I. Complete with what looked like direct quotes from both of our parents.

"She's going to flip. And completely deny it," I said.

"Maybe not. She might think twice about doing that when she sees how happy everyone is for her, for us. She won't want to go against all her followers or do anything that would make her look bad. She'll have no choice but to accept us. To accept me in your life."

"Do you think it will work?" I asked.

"It already has," Jay said and showed me all the comments on the post.

"See, she has replied back. 'Thank you so much. The whole family is just thrilled,' or how about, 'Yes. I will make a beautiful mother of the bride.' The comments go on and on and on. She's going to love the attention so much so she'll have to give in. If she backs out it will look bad on her. Not on us"

"Do you really think it will work?" I asked. I didn't want to be hopeful, but Jay was making me feel this would succeed.

"There's only one way to find out. If nothing else, it will buy us some time. Plus, I think I know the reason your mother is the way she is."

"She's a sad, angry, bitter woman?" I asked.

"Well, that too. But I think she still has feelings for my dad. That she never got over him. That she was doing this as much so that she could get his attention. So maybe by us getting married, they will have to spend time together and they can patch things up."

"Do you think your father would be open to that? Do you think he still cares for my mom?" I asked.

"Maybe. But we're going to find out," he said.

"Okay. That's great and all but there's one big thing that you forgot about," I said and glared at him.

"No. No. I didn't. I know this isn't the way you want it to be. And it isn't the way I wanted it to be. But if we have to have an unconventional proposal just so that I can keep you in my life, then I will do a nonconventional proposal, wedding, anniversary, baby showers, birthday parties, whatever I have to do. As long as I get to have you in my life. I love you; I want to spend the rest of my life with you. I want you to be my wife, I want to be your husband. If it's too soon to propose, I'll wait. You tell me when you're ready and I will give you the best most amazing proposal in the world. For the rest of the world we can just say we are having a long engagement. All that matters, is that you're happy, and you get what you want and that you're okay with all of this. I know I should have asked you before I did all this, but I was so excited I just wanted to do it. And I wanted to get in front of your mother before she did something. I never thought it would take off the way it did. But, if it allows us to be together, then I'm okay with it. If you're okay with it."

"Was that your proposal?" I asked. I was so happy I could burst. Not only had Jay found a way for us to be together, but he was also practically proposing to me. I didn't know how to tell him I didn't care how he did it. I just wanted him. Instead, I thought it would be fun to make him squirm a little.

"No. Of course not. I will do it way better when you let me," he said.

"Are you saying you don't want to propose to me?" I asked.

"No. I want to marry you. I will marry you tomorrow if you would let me. My life is with you. My life is you. It has been since the moment I saw you again. I love you."

"Good then, yes. I will marry you," I said.

"Wait? What?" He asked, clearly confused.

"I love that you want to do something special that you need to make it memorable for us. But I don't need that. I love you. Of course, I want to marry you. No, this isn't the way I would have thought it would happen, but you have the rest of our lives to make it up to me. And for me to show you how happy I am that you're mine. I don't want this to be a pretend engagement. I don't want to wait for another time for you to propose to me. I want to be your wife, as soon as possible. I want the rest of our lives together to start right now. All I care about is being with you," I said.

"Willow. You're amazing. I love you. I promise to make the wedding and our lives the best ever."

"You already have by simply being there," I said to him and went into his arms.

Epilogue

Jay

"Jay! Willow! Over here!"

I kept my hand firmly on the small of Willow's back and turned to look at the gaggle of photographers.

"Keep smiling," I said through my teeth to Willow.

"I am," she said back in the same manner. I could feel how tense she was.

"It's almost over," I said to her.

We slowly worked our way down the red carpet. Smiling at the photographers and even doing a few interviews with reporters before we moved our way inside the lobby of the theatre. It was only then that she and I relaxed. We stepped away from the crowd to admire the decorations and the other people who were there.

"Is that?" Willow asked.

"Yes," I said when I saw who she was gawking at.

"I can't believe we're here. Surrounded by so many celebrities, that all those reporters wanted to talk to you. It's all so surreal."

I agreed with her. I had thought I knew what to expect when my movie did well and was up for numerous awards, but I had never thought it would be to the extent that it was. It had been a whirlwind of parties, awards shows, presentations, and interviews. It had been an insane six months. But through it all, Willow had been by my side. Supporting me, loving me, grounded me and looking more beautiful than all the other celebrities combined.

"You look amazing," I said to Willow.

She blushed and looked down at her black full length dress. "Thanks. I feel like a princess at a ball."

"You look like one too. Thank you for doing this. For being there for me. For going on this crazy ride with me," I said.

"There's nowhere else I would rather be. Well, maybe at home curled up watching a movie with you. But as long as I'm with you, I'm good. I'm better than good. I'm perfect."

"Yes, you are. You're perfect. In every way," I said.

"Stop," she said and patted my chest.

"You know I couldn't have done this without you. That I wouldn't be here without you. That everything that has happened is because you were there for me, beside me, supporting and loving me every step of the way."

"I love you. I want you to succeed," she said.

To her, it was that simple. It had been for us since the night at Kayla's apartment. We had gone out the next day and I had bought her a ring, which was actually a lot of fun to shop with her for. As I had predicted, her mother had needed to pretend to be happy about our engagement and hadn't objected in public. In private, she continued to try and break us up, but I should have realized it was as much so that she could get my father to defend us. He was all for Willow and I getting married and whenever Stephanie would make a comment or try and sabotage us, he stepped in.

They had bickered constantly right up until the wedding. Willow and I just laughed through it. We could see that they both cared about each other and were too stubborn to say anything. We were too happy to be with each other, to be getting married that they couldn't dampen our joy and excitement. It also didn't surprise us to see my father come out of Stephanie's room the morning after the wedding.

Willow and I had moved up to San Francisco where she now was the head paralegal for Smith, Hargrove, and Associates. My career had taken off and I found that being with her and in San Francisco made me more creative. I already had finished two other screenplays that were being optioned by two top movie companies. I had wanted to get them done as soon as possible as Willow and I were going to have another addition to our family soon.

"I want us both to succeed and to be happy," I said.

"As long as I have you and our baby," she said and put her hand protectively on top of her stomach, "then I'm happy."

"Me too," I said and kissed her.

"Shall we?" she asked.

"Yes," I said and took her hand in mine and walked into the theatre.

THE END

Turn the page for a preview the next book in

My Stepbrother Series:

My Stepbrother, My Best Friend.

Sofia:

Cole could have any woman he wanted.

So why would he want me?

But I can't ignore the looks, the smiles, the filtration.

Nor the mind numbing kiss that leaves my knees weak.

Could he really want to be with me?

Could we really have a future?

Cole:

Sofia and I have known each other forever.

She has always been the good girl and I've been the bad boy.

It was a relationship that worked well for both of us.

That was until I found myself attracted to her.

Now I have no idea what to do with a woman.

When she matters more than anyone before.

"Good game," he said as we put our putters away.

"Yes, it was. Especially because I won," I teased.

"There will be a rematch. You already agreed," he said.

"That I did. But first, bumper boats," I said.

"Lead on milady," Cole said and bent down into a deep bow.

I shook my head at him as I walked past him and to the bumper boats. They were off to the far end of the family fun center. Behind the Ferris Wheel and roller coaster but right next to the batting cages. There was a small circular pond with rows of bumper boats lined along the edges. They had just finished a round of people, so the boats were all sitting idle waiting for the next group. There looked to be only a small amount of people waiting for the next round.

"Come on, let's hurry. Maybe we can get into the next group," Cole said to me and charged past me.

I followed quickly behind him and got up to him right as he was paying for two tickets.

"You didn't have to do that," I said.

"Yes. I did. I told you I was going to buy the bumper boats. You were too quick for me to get the miniature golf," he said.

"Fine. Plus, maybe I was hoping this would be the favor you would ask for," he added.

"I'm not going to waste my favor on you paying for something you already agreed to. Now, if I had gotten here before you, then maybe I could have gotten another favor out of you," I said.

"Ah, you think that's how it works?" he asked.

"A girl can try," I said.

"Not going to happen. Nor is your winning streak. Prepared to be soaked," he said and took our tickets.

"It's so cute how you think you're better at this than I am. Every time we've gone here, you leave soaked, and I am perfectly dry."

"Well, today is the day that all changes," he said and handed our tickets to the guy at the gate.

We quickly found our boats; I liked to take the one with the green flag while Cole always chose one with a blue. After we were checked that we were securely in our seats and given some brief instructions we took off. Cole always liked to go for the immediate soak, and that day was no exception. As soon as we were both in the water, he took after me, gunning for me. I could see him coming and easily avoided him. I laughed as he gave me a dirty look. It only egged me on to get away from him and to try and work the perfect strategy to get him.

I took my time, working around other boaters, and getting the occasional splash. I watched from across the way when he let a young girl soak him with her boat. The squeal of laughter from her could be heard throughout the park. Cole took it all in stride and gave her air high five as he motored away from her. While he was moving, it gave me the perfect opportunity to get him. I could tell he didn't know where I was and was looking around trying to find me. He turned his boat around a split second before I splashed him. Soaking him and the boat. Before he had time to react, I had already moved away. Cole lifted his hand up in frustration, and I only laughed.

We felt more like our usual selves again. Laughing and teasing each other as we spent the remainder of the time with him trying to get me and failing miserably. With a look, we were able to gang up on the little girl that had soaked him, blocking her in so that Cole could hit her again. She laughed hysterically when we did and then she and I ganged up on Cole to soak him one more time.

By the time we brought our boats back, Cole was as soaked and I was still relatively dry.

"Look at me," he said as we met up near the entrance. "I'm soaked through the bone."

"I told you, you would be," I said.

"That isn't fair. Come here. I need a hug, I'm sad," he said and tried to reach for me.

"Oh no, you don't!" I said and squirmed away from him.

"Daddy! Daddy! Look how wet I am!" the little girl from before said as she ran up to her dad.

"Yes. I see. Did you have fun?" he asked.

"The best! Can I go again?" she asked.

"Maybe next weekend," he said and then looked up at Cole and I and nodded at us. Thanking us without words for making his daughter happy.

We walked past them, and Cole went to try and dry himself off. I walked over to the batting cages and watched some people hit the balls for a few minutes. The bumper boats had helped to salvage the day. It reminded me of the fun we used to have when we were in college. Cole and I had started playing miniature golf and going on the bumper boats after a particular long midterm week. Both of us were burnt out, hating that we were getting older and were worried that we would never be able to have the fun that we had when we were kids.

Cole, forever a man with an excellent idea, decided to change that and suggested we go do something frivolous. It became a tradition to do this after every midterm and final. I looked forward to the tests as much for when they were done Cole and I would do this. It was what had started us become such good friends. As the years progressed and we continued to do it, other friends wanted to join in on the fun, but neither Cole or I would let them. It was only for us.

As I walked back to the bumper boats, I knew that the time for just Cole and I was ending. That we were indeed growing up and that things were going to change. Who knew when we would be able to get back to this again. If ever. I knew that if we never did, that I had this day. This wonderful memory of us to last me. As I turned the corner, it was to see Cole talking to a group of women. Just like at the bar the other night, he was laughing and flirting and looking like he was having the time of his life. He looked so relaxed, so in his element that I felt a sharp pain in my heart.

Of course, he would. That was where he belonged. Being surrounded by people who loved him, who adored him, who would worship him and think he was the best guy in the world. Not some woman that he was friends with out of pity and I was starting to see that was the case. He was only being nice to me because he had to, or he felt some strange obligation to me. I should have seen it sooner, and now that I did, I knew that I needed to end our friendship.

I had tried to fight my feelings, to think that I could be okay being just friends with him, but I knew I couldn't. And I wasn't going to stand by and watch him fall in love with another woman, have kids with her, buy a house with her and live happily ever after. It would be too hard for me. I knew I couldn't just never talk to him again, though for me that would have been the easiest thing. I needed to spend less and less time with him, slowly. It was what would happen anyway; it just would be easier for me to do if I was the one doing it. Not through time and circumstances.

Standing off to the side I began to wonder if one of the women he was talking to would be the one who would win his heart and if they had any idea how lucky they would be if they did.

Cole must have sensed me standing off to the side for he turned, and his eyes immediately fell on me. My heart leaped in my throat as he did, and I had to stop myself from imaging what it would be like if he looked at me first all the time. That the smile he sent me meant more than friendship.

He slowly stepped away from the women, and I could see his hesitation. That he didn't want to go and I almost called to him that he should stay, have some fun. I needed to get back and study. But I wanted the night to continue. I wanted to enjoy all the last moments with him that I could. There would be a lady who would monopolize his time soon enough, and I would be a distant memory. For now, I wanted to enjoy what he and I had. Even if I knew it was all going to end.

"There you are," he said.

"I got distracted watching the people in the batting cages," I said.

"Remembering your days of softball?" he asked.

"A little," I said.

"You up for some dinner?" he asked.

"I'm starving," I said.

"Good. Me too," he replied, and we walked across the street to Tally's, one of our favorite burger joints.

I grabbed us a table as Cole went up and ordered for us. We had been there enough times that he knew exactly what I wanted and how I liked it. We were both hungry, and the burgers, onion rings, and shakes were gone in no time. As we ate, we reminisced about the other times we had gone to Tally's and all the times we had come to the fun center. It was wonderful to listen to him tell the stories, to hear them from his perspective to laugh with him about all the adventures that we had. It only showed me how much I had and how much I was going to miss him when we didn't talk or hang out.

As much as it was going to hurt, I knew it was for the best. That I needed to let him go. Not only for his sake but for mine. I could see that I was a crutch that was bringing him down, that he shouldn't have to do that anymore. Our time together had been amazing, some of the best years of my life, but it was time for both of us to move on. To linger any longer would only make it worse later on and I couldn't do that. I wouldn't do that.

It was dark as we exited the restaurant and started walking towards my car. It was getting chilly out but not so much that I needed a jacket.

"That was a lovely evening, but I can't wait for the rematch and hopefully earn some of my dignity back," he teased.

"You never lost your dignity, and you won't get it back when I kick your ass again."

"Well, that's the only way that I might be able to win that favor," he said.

I had been thinking about the favor, as he called it, all night. I knew what I wanted from him; I just didn't know if I could actually ask him for it. But I knew if I didn't ask, I would never get a chance to again. It could be my parting gift from Cole. Something that I could take with me so that I could remember him always.

"Speaking of that favor," I said.

"Oh, have you decided what you want for yours?" he asked. He stopped between a row of cars, not far from my car, crossed his arms, and looked at me.

He was looking at me with such interested that I could feel myself blush.

"Are you blushing? This has got to be good," he said.

"Cole," I said and then stopped. I couldn't get the words out. I wanted to, but I couldn't.

"Yes. What do you want? Just tell me Sofia," he said.

His words sent shivers down my spine. He said my name so softly, almost seductively, I was shocked and excited. I started to hope again that maybe he did care about me as more than a friend. It gave me the courage to say what was in my heart.

"Would you kiss me?" I asked.

My heart was in my throat, my breath held as I waited for him to answer. He looked at me so sweetly. Tilting his head slightly and looking at me so intently I felt like he was looking into my soul. I couldn't move as he slowly reached his hands up to my face. Cupping it in his palms. They felt warm and vibrant, and he locked his eyes on mine as he moved his lips closer to me.

My eyes closed, and my mouth opened slightly. I was overwhelmed by the thought that he was going to kiss me. That I was going to know what it felt like to feel his body pressed up against mine. To feel our tongues move around each other. To hold him in my arms. But before he touched his lips to mine, I could feel him tense up. My eyes shot open, and I gave him a confused look.

As his hands slipped away from my face, I could feel him stepping away from me. Not only physically, but emotionally and mentally as well. I stepped away from him as he whispered, "I can't."

I quickly turned away from him. I didn't want him to see me cry. I didn't want him to see how much what he said hurt me.

"That's fine. It was a stupid idea. I don't know what I was thinking. Thanks for a great night. I should be going," I said over my shoulder.

"Sofia! Wait," Cole said as I started to walk away.

I didn't stop; I didn't turn around. I only wanted to get into my car and drive as fast and as far away from Cole and never see him again.

To read more, go to Amazon

10678489R00104